DEFLECTED

M.E. CARTER

First Edition: December 2018
Library of Congress Cataloging-in-Publication Data
Deflected – 1st ed
ISBN-13: 978-1-948852-15-9

To all the Texas Mutiny fans—
As we close out an era, know that I have immense gratitude to all
of you for your love of a soccer team and the relationships that go
with it.

CHAPTER 1

Tiffany

Something jars me from my sleep, but I'm comfortable enough, I don't care to figure out what it is. The air in the room is cool, but the body behind me is warm. The contrast in temperatures is perfect, so I snuggle right back down into my pillows and doze off.

Until I'm jarred from my sleep. Again.

"Why the hell is your phone going off at the butt crack of dawn?" Rowen's voice sounds groggy and muffled from the blankets.

"It's not that early. It's"—I lean over to look at the clock—"8:06. Okay, yeah. That's early."

He pulls me back down for more snuggles. "Stop moving. I'm comfortable."

I let him resituate us, my little spoon fitting perfectly

against his big spoon. I love sleeping next to him. He makes me feel safe and insulated from the world. Plus, that whole body heat thing.

My comfort is short-lived when my phone goes off *again*.

"Son of a bitch," I grumble and untangle myself from the blankets, reaching for my phone. "What do you want to bet it's Quincy, freaking out about my hair appointment this morning?"

"Why did you schedule a hair appointment the morning after we got back from our honeymoon?"

"I didn't know it was going to be our honeymoon. You sort of sprung that whole wedding thing on me, remember?"

It was actually pretty perfect. After being the focal point of one of the biggest sports scandals ever to hit US professional soccer, I am more than happy to never be the center of attention again. Especially since it was a naked picture of me that made its way around the World Wide Web. I knew before we left for Fiji that Rowen was it for me. I just didn't expect him to propose and marry me the same night. Turns out, he knew exactly what I'd want, and a private ceremony, just him and me—no family, no paparazzi, no stress—was exactly the way I needed it to be.

"Oh, I definitely remember getting married. And our wedding night." Rowen begins a trek of kisses from my shoulder down my arm. "The thought of jet lag never crossed your mind?"

I try to ignore his lips on my skin, but it's damn near impossible. The man is insatiable. "Nope. It was the first time I've been out of the country. Never occurred to me." I blink my eyes, trying to get them to focus on the tiny little words on my text messages. "And I always make my hair appointment for the morning. That way I can get it done before work. I didn't even think about it."

Finally, the words on the screen come into focus.

Quincy: *Are you still coming in today?*

Quincy: *Tiffany, wake up so you're here on time!*

Quincy: *I'm serious. It's a hair emergency! We're doing all-over color, right?*

"What the hell?" I grumble. "What the hell is a hair emergency?"

"Hmm?" Rowen mumbles as he continues his journey with his lips.

"Nothing. Quincy's being weird."

Me: *Relax, you psycho. I'll be there. And yes, all-over color.*

"You work today?"

"No." I toss my phone back on the nightstand, knowing I'm not getting out of this bed without having at least one orgasm. "Just my hair appointment, and then I'm free all day.

"Good." Rowen's hand slides down my thigh, and he nudges my legs apart. "Open." I lift my top leg to give him complete access to me. His finger slides inside and he moves it back and forth, thrusting in and out, and we both groan. "I have no idea how I lived without this for so long."

"I don't know, but I'm so glad you did."

Suddenly, his finger is gone, and his cock takes its place. I groan again. He feels so good. This is exactly where I want him to be.

For someone who stayed a virgin until our wedding night,

Rowen has proven to be quite the adventurer in bed. He likes trying different positions and locations… he's not an exhibitionist, though. He's still extremely protective over my virtue, unless he's the one violating it, of course. But we could probably write our own Kama Sutra book with things no one has ever seen before. For a girl who has always loved sex, having a husband who loves it just as much is a dream come true. Don't get me wrong, I would still be happily married even if he didn't have such a high libido. But I won't ever complain about how much sex I get.

I anchor myself with my hand and grind my hips against his every time he thrusts. Quickly, we discover this is a nice position, but it doesn't get him as deep as we like it.

Rowen pulls out and sits up on his knees, the sheets falling off of us. The crisp air makes my nipples harden even more than they were before. Positioning himself behind me, he gently lifts my top leg again and drives inside me. I raise my hips, causing him to get deeper. His fingers are digging into my hip and thigh as he thrusts.

"You okay?" he asks gently, continuing his movements.

"Oh yeah. This is better. It feels good, babe."

I twist my body to look at him over my shoulder and smile. His thighs flex, his chest strains tight as he hangs on to my hips for dear life. I turn back and anchor myself again, raising my hips ever so slightly once more.

My breathing picks up as his cock hits that spot deep inside me.

"Keep doing that, Rowen," I breathe. "Just a little harder."

He complies and pushes deeper still, hitting me just the right way.

"Right there, Rowen… ooooooohhhhh…" My entire body

feels like it lights up as my orgasm shoots through me.

Behind me, Rowen's movements get jerky as he begins to climax. "Oh god. Oh fuck, babe."

I lose track of how long he comes, too sated from my own pleasure. Eventually, he practically melts on top of me as he comes down from his high. Kissing his way up my arm, over my shoulder, around my neck, across my jaw…

I put my hand on his mouth to stop him. "Morning breath. Don't kiss me."

"I don't give a damn about morning breath," he practically growls.

"I do. I want to live with the fantasy that my husband is perfect in every way. I don't want to know about any hygiene issues yet."

He props himself up on his elbow to look at me. "You suck my cock and have this random fascination with my butthole, but you're worried about my morning breath?"

I giggle. "One time, Rookie. I lightly brushed your ass one time with my finger, and you would've thought I set your butt on fire."

He settles back in behind me. "Exit only, baby."

"I know. And I don't want to know anything about what comes out of there either."

He chuckles. "You realize someday you're going to have to brush your teeth or pee or something right after I shit, right? You're going to find out it smells like everyone else's."

"Someday. But for now, I'm pretending you smell like roses." I kiss his hand and throw the covers off of me. "I'm gonna be late."

"Hey," he gripes, "it's cold."

Clamoring out of bed, the covers are barely back over him when he snuggles into the pillows.

I jump in the shower to wash off the smell of sex, even though I love his scent on me. But Quincy probably won't appreciate getting up close and personal with it, so his body wash will just have to suffice today.

Forty-five minutes later, I've kissed my husband goodbye, driven to the salon, and am still barely coherent while being manhandled by Quincy.

"Ohmygod, I'm so happy to see you! Congratulations!" She releases me from the world's tightest hug and grabs my hand. "Oh wow! Look at that rock! He did so good! It's beautiful!" Grabbing my hand, Quincy drags me to her station. She wasn't kidding when she said she'd be prepared before I got there. All her supplies are sitting out on a tray, waiting for her to mix and apply. "How was the trip? Was it amazing?" She shakes out the cape and wraps it around my neck.

"It was beautiful," I say with a smile. "It would've been better if I wasn't woken up first thing this morning to frantic texts."

She looks sheepish. "Sorry about that. I have to squeeze someone in while your color processes. She's having a hair emergency."

"I got that from your messages, but what does that mean?"

Quincy blows out a breath, like it's quite the dramatic story. "My client's five-year-old granddaughter and her parents are staying with her for a few days."

"Uh huh."

"Apparently the granddaughter decided overnight she wants to be a hair dresser."

"Oh no." I have a bad feeling I know where this is going.

"Yeah. She woke up this morning to a new set of bangs."

My eyes widen. "Oh no! The little girl gave herself

bangs?"

She shakes her head and tightens her jaw, like she's trying really hard not to find it funny. "No. She gave *my client* bangs."

I gasp.

"Yep. The worst part is they're visiting because they have a family wedding to go to tonight. Which means family pictures they'll be in. And I have no idea if I'll be able to fix it."

"Are you talking about Sue again?" Geni, another stylist, guesses, plopping into her chair and grabbing a magazine. "I told her that child was a hellion."

"She's not that bad," Quincy quips.

"Sue has new bangs; that says she is." Geni keeps flipping through the magazine, absent-mindedly. "Anyway, how are you feeling now, Whore?" She turns to address me. "You're looking kind of tired. Your man keeping you up late at night?"

"Geni!" Quincy reprimands.

"What? You think she's been staying up late playing cards?" Geni leans forward as she asks for details. "How is he? A ferocious tiger in the sack? A gentle lover? Give me details."

"I'm not giving you details, Slutbag." Somehow insults have become our thing. We trade them back and forth constantly. The stranger, the better. "What happens in the privacy of my bedroom, stays there."

She snorts. "You're full of shit."

"I'm serious! It's different now that I'm married. It's more… I don't know… intimate. I like it that way."

Geni rolls her eyes. "Fine. I can respect that. For now. But next time you're drunk, I need to know how he compares to the others."

"Deal," I answer, knowing full well I won't be drinking

around her any time soon. With any luck, she'll forget all about this conversation by then.

"Tell us more about this wedding anyway," Quincy says, as she twists part of my hair up and out of the way. "The pictures looked fabulous."

"Pictures?" My heart starts beating wildly. "What pictures?"

"The pictures online."

My breathing picks up, and I know I just went pale. Ever since that picture of me was put out for the entire first world to see, I've been adamant that my private life stays private. Nothing gets released without my approval first. No pictures. No information. Nothing. To this day, I don't know who took the nudie pic of me, so now Rowen and I are very, very careful who knows about our everyday lives or sees us in pictures. Even our wedding pictures.

"I didn't give anyone permission to post a picture online," I whisper, my hands balling into fists. I feel like I'm about to lose it.

Geni stills, and Quincy catches my eyes in the mirror.

"Relax," she says quietly, putting a hand on my shoulder. "It was only one, and it's a nice picture."

"Are you sure?" I know it's ridiculous that I'm freaking out. But when your privacy has been violated in such a humiliating and public way, stuff like this can trigger some very unwelcome feelings.

"Here, babe," Geni says, squatting down in front of me, holding her phone out for me to see. "It was this one. It's beautiful."

When I finally focus, I realize it's actually my favorite picture from that night. The beautiful blue ocean in the background, the bouquet of native flowers held close to my thigh, my dark hair over one shoulder. Rowen's forehead rests against my head, a small smile on his lips, and I'm looking at the camera.

I nod and take a deep breath. "You're sure that's the only one?"

Geni looks at me kindly, which she doesn't do often and means she knows how badly I am freaking out right now. She gives me a reassuring smile. "I'm the biggest bitch you know. Would I be standing here calmly if there was something else you didn't know about?"

She's got a point. When she gets mad, she's a mass of inappropriate language and empty threats.

I relax a little. "How the hell did that picture get released? We didn't give it to anyone except his parents and—" I stop abruptly when it all comes together.

"What?" Quincy asks, pausing momentarily mid stroke.

"My mother."

"You think it was her?"

"I know it was her. Wait… how did you guys find out we got married, anyway?"

Quincy looks at me like I'm ridiculous. "When we saw the picture. How did you think we found out?"

"Honestly, I thought Rowen must've texted Daniel. It never occurred to me he'd be able to keep it a secret. He's not very good at that when he's excited."

She laughs. "Yeah, those guys are the biggest gossips. And they accuse us of talking too much."

"Please. We gossip at the hair salon once every six to eight weeks. They do it in the locker room every day."

"Seriously." She grabs more color on her brush and continues painting my hair. "Tell us about this wedding anyway. Do you have any more pictures?"

So I tell them the whole story. From Rowen proposing on the beach to him having wedding dresses delivered to the hotel for me to try on to saying our "I do's" at sunset. It feels nice to tell people I trust, who are genuinely interested in my wedding, and not because they're going to post it online. I briefly wonder if I'll ever fully get over the scandal.

"Okay, let's get you under the dryers," Quincy says as she throws the brushes in the now empty bowls. "Looks like Sue is here."

I look over and see an older woman wearing a hoodie and dark sunglasses.

Geni chuckles. "Oh yes. That's inconspicuous."

"Don't make fun," Quincy says as she pushes the tray of supplies to the side. "She's you in about fifty years."

"Hey!" Geni cries then stops to think. "Yeah, okay. That's accurate." She shrugs, turning to go get her own client who just arrived.

Quincy gets me situated under the dryer and leaves me with my phone for entertainment. As much as I want to look up the most recent sports scores, I need to text my mom first.

Me: *Good morning, Mom. I have a question.*

Mom: *Hi Honey! Glad to see you're back in the land of the living.*

Me: *Barely. I've never had jet lag. It's worse that I imagined it would be.*

Mom: *Aw. I'm sorry. What's up? You and my new son-in-law getting back into the swing of things?*

Me: *Working on it. Hey, did you release a wedding pic to the press?*

Mom: *No, of course not! I put a wedding announce-ment in the paper. But only in Nashville and Detroit for the families to see.*

I groan. My mother still doesn't seem to understand that anything related to Rowen won't stay local news. Ever. I didn't even realize how far Rowen's reach was until we went to Los Angeles last year for one of his games. As we left the restaurant where we had dinner, some European tourists recognized him. It took me a minute to finally catch the word "Ryan" as the tourists chatted back and forth while taking pictures with us. That's when I finally put it all together…

Soccer has a huge international following. It's arguably bigger than football is in the States.

Ryan Flanigan, Rowen's dad, is a legend in the European Premier League. Think David Beckham on a larger scale. Thus anything to do with Ryan is a big deal. And Rowen is his son. Therefore, he's a big, big deal in Europe.

Me: *Okay. Just wanted to make sure.*

Mom: *No problem. I've gotten more compliments about how beautiful that picture is.*

Me: *Me too, Ma. I'll call you when I have more time.*

Mom: *Okay, sweetie. Love you.*

Me: *Love you too.*

I look up and over at Quincy's station. The older woman no longer has a hoodie and sunglasses on. And it's easy to tell neither of them is happy about the situation. Even from here I can see those bangs are going to be really hard to fix. This is why I'm okay with not having kids for a while. Later, when I'm older and have the time and desire to monitor their every move, sure. But not now. I'm too selfish right now and not too proud to admit that.

My phone vibrates in my hand, and I look down to see a text from Rowen.

Rowen: *Babe. Apparently one of the pics from the wedding is out there. Don't freak out. I've googled everything I can think of and it's only one.*

Me: *I know. I was just about to text you. Apparently my mother thought it was nice for the families to have a wedding announcement in each of our hometowns.*

Rowen: *Thank god. I was afraid I was going to have to raise hell with the photographer or the hotel.*

Me: *Nope. Good ol' mom still hasn't figured out what the word "privacy" means.*

Rowen: *I'm sorry, babe. You okay with all this?*

Me: *I'm fine. Not thrilled but nothing I can do about it.*

Rowen: *I can do something to take your mind off it when you get home. ;)*

I chuckle to myself. He's insatiable. I love it.

Me: *I bet you can. I'll see you when I get done.*

I spend the next several minutes scrolling through sports scores and seeing if there's anything major I missed while we were gone and make a mental note to remind Steve that the Cowboys are coming to town in a couple weeks. Before I know it, Quincy's ready for me again, has me shampooed, and is leading me back at her station.

"How'd it go with the bangs?"

She shoots me a glare as she picks up her scissors. "I told her to stand in the back row for all the pictures."

"It's not an outdoor wedding, it is?"

"Nope. And I already suggested a hat."

I smirk and watch as she combs through my hair.

"I have a favor to ask," she says, switching gears.

"Hit me."

"Do you want to come over tonight and help me pack? That one over there"—she gestures towards Geni, who holds her hands up like she's innocent—"just sits around and watches while I do everything, and I have to be out of the apartment by the end of next week."

"I keep an eye on the baby for you, and then we watch *Outlander*," Geni challenges.

"That's a load of crap and you know it." Quincy points her scissors Geni's direction. "Well, maybe not the *Outlander* part. I can't help my love for Jamie Fraser."

"Why does Tiffany need to watch *Outlander* with us when she has her own hot dude with a brogue at home?"

I open my mouth to speak but realize she's right.

Quincy freezes mid cut. "Rowen doesn't happen to have a kilt, does he?"

"I don't know the answer to that. Do Irish men wear kilts or is it just a Scottish thing?"

"There's a lot of debate about when Ireland adopted the tradition of wearing kilts, but it could have been several hundred years ago," Geni spits out, as she runs the clippers over her client's neck.

Quincy and I just stare at her.

"What?" Geni shrugs. "I know things."

We keep staring.

"Plus, kilts are hot, so I looked it up."

Quincy and I nod like that answer makes more sense. And I make a mental note to ask Rowen about this. Geni's right. My husband in a kilt could be seriously hot.

"Anyway," Quincy says, breaking me away from the visual images running through my brain. "I know it's short notice, but I figured with the poker game tonight, you might not have anything to do."

So much for staying in and letting my new husband ravish me all over again. "Poker night is tonight?"

"Yeah, Christian made this big deal about Daniel never having another one once the baby and I move in, so they're doing it tonight."

"I'll double check with Rowen, but I'm guessing I can come over."

"Yay! Maybe I'll actually get something done now."

"I heard that," Geni complains.

"I wasn't hiding it from you," Quincy retorts.

I unravel my arms from behind the cape and text Rowen.

Me: *Apparently poker night is tonight.*

Rowen: *I just heard.*

Me: *I take it you're going?*

Rowen: *Under duress.*

Me: *Okay. I'll hang out at Quincy's while you're there.*

Rowen: *Sounds like a plan. Not a fun one, but a plan, anyway.*

I snigger. I'm really happy with the friends we've ended up with. But I wish we could have stayed in that newlywed bubble for a little longer.

CHAPTER 2

Rowen

I glance over at my wife as we drive down the highway to Daniel's apartment. A glow passes over her face every time a street light goes by and I catch glimpses of her lips. Those lips were wrapped around my cock a couple hours ago. The thought of her on her knees, the round of her naked ass visible every time I looked down, while she gave me head makes me shift in my seat to relieve the pressure off my dick.

"Eyes on the road, Rookie," she says without looking up from her phone.

I chuckle. "Sorry." She tosses her cell on the floor when she's done, and I grab her hand, entwining our fingers and laying them on her thigh. My thumb makes lazy circles on the soft skin of her leg. When she shivers, I have to shift again.

"You're making it really hard for me to enjoy tonight when you touch me like that."

"Who's trying to be happy? I'm still pissed I got suckered into going."

"Oh, come on," she says with a grin as I turn into the parking lot of Daniel's complex. "It'll be fun to get together with your friends. Plus, after spending all that money on a vacation, I need you to clean them out."

"I plan to." By nature, I'm a people-watcher. Sometimes, it makes me have more insight than I want into other people's lives. But on poker night, I can take advantage of it by figuring out everyone's tells. "It'll serve them right for taking me away from my wife."

"I love it when you call me that."

Pulling into the indicated space and shifting the car into park, I lean over and cup Tiffany's face, bringing her mouth to mine. She immediately parts her lips to allow me entrance, and my tongue dives in, taking what I want and reminding her of what she's got all to herself.

A few heavy make-out minutes later, we break apart.

"What was that for?" She's breathing heavily, and it makes me happy knowing I made her breathless.

"Just a quick reminder of what you have waiting for you. You know. Just so you don't stay too long at Quincy's watching Starz."

Climbing out of the car, we immediately reach for each other as we head for the stairs to Daniel's second-story apartment.

"Speaking of Starz, do you have a kilt?"

I look at her quizzically. "What does one have to do with the other?"

She smirks. "Oh, just something Geni was saying today

about that show *Outlander* and some argument over Irish versus Scottish kilts."

I groan. "That dumb show has gotten all the women riled up about what we wear underneath."

"So, you do have one?" Her eyes light up, and she gets a little bounce in her step as she tugs on my arm. "Is it at home?"

"I'm sure there's one at my parents' house, if they still have it." Tiffany deflates a little, which makes me chuckle. "We almost never wear them. My grandfather did, but that was actually in Ireland. Not Detroit. But if you're into role playing or something"—I pop her on the ass as she climbs the stairs in front of me, making her squeal—"I'll find one and wear it just for you."

She turns around and puts her hands on my shoulders. Leaning in, she kisses me slowly. "But will you tell me what you're wearing underneath?" I can feel her smiling against my lips.

"A man has to have some secrets," I banter then kiss her again. "You'll just have to find out for *yerself.*" She has me worked up enough now, my accent bleeds through.

"Poker night cannot be over soon enough," she grumbles, grabbing my hand and pulling me the rest of the way to the apartment.

Her phone buzzes in her pocket as I knock. Before she can unlock the screen, Christian flings the door wide open.

"It's the Flanigans!" He hauls Tiffany in for a hug, a huge grin on his face, then yanks me in for one as well. "She did it, Rookie. She finally made an honest man out of you," he razzes, wrapping his arm around my neck and dragging me into the other room. I try to turn around for Tiffany, but she calls out behind me.

"I'm coming. Just texting Quincy back."

"Speak of the devil," Christian continues to joke, and I know we've been the topic of conversation. "Look who finally got his cherry popped. Does he look different to you?"

I know I turn beet red as he pretends to look me over. It happens every time I'm embarrassed or upset. I respond like any man would, I start throwing fake punches, which, as always, leads to a wrestling match between the two of us.

"Hey! No WAGs allowed tonight," Luca exclaims as he makes his way into the room. I break away from Christian, fake fighting forgotten, when I hear Tiffany respond.

"Don't mind me, guys. I'm just here to pick up some boxes for Quincy."

"Oh yeah. Let me get those." Daniel jumps up from his seat and heads down the hall.

Everyone else is opening bags of chips and lighting up cigars… your basic poker night shit. They all seem relaxed and carefree. Except Santos. Santos is radiating anger. I ignore him, hoping Tiffany doesn't notice. The guy still blames everyone else and their mother for his problems.

Randall leans back in his chair, oblivious to the boiling pot sitting next to him. "Seriously guys, congratulations. Rebecca was jealous you guys got hitched in Fiji. Says I need to take her there to get our vows renewed, or something."

I kiss Tiffany on the top of the head as she puts her arm around my waist. "You should," she says with a smile. "Fiji is just beautiful. And not just the way they do a wedding. I could live there. It's unlike anything I've ever seen."

Suddenly, Santos shoves his chair away from the table and stomps into the kitchen. The room goes silent. I vaguely notice Tiffany look at her phone again, too busy gauging the reactions of the rest of my teammates.

"Don't worry about him," Sammy asserts as he pours some Scotch in a glass. "He's just having a rough go of it."

"Um," Tiffany flashes her phone to me. "I'll be right back. I have to get something out of the kitchen for Quincy." I cock my head at her in question. She smiles and puts her hand on my forearm. "It's okay. I just have to get some red washcloth or something."

"Did she forget that?" Daniel questions as he walks back in the room, holding some boxes. "Chance won't go to sleep without that thing. It's weird what babies get attached to."

"You mean like that baby doll you used to carry around as a kid?" Christian chides while everyone laughs.

"First of all, quit getting my mama to show you all my baby pictures. She's a sucker for that shit and you know it." Daniel tosses the boxes on the couch and sits down at the table. "Second, it wasn't a doll. It was a Munchichi. And he was cool."

I reach for my chair, but before I can sit, there's yelling in the kitchen and words like "fucking groupie whore" are being tossed out.

"What the fuck?" I hear behind me as I bolt for the door. Swinging it open, I see Tiffany standing wide-eyed, Santos yelling in her face.

"You don't belong here. Do you hear me? *She* deserves to be here. *You* don't."

"Back. The fuck off. My wife. Before this gets any uglier."

"Oh shit," someone says behind me as I move into the room and the door closes. Santos's eyes snap over to mine, and Tiffany immediately moves to my side. I have never been this angry in my life. It is taking everything in me to hold back. "Babe, I think you need go to the other room."

"Rowen," Tiffany argues, "it's okay. I get why he's angry."

I take my eyes off Santos's to look at her. We've had this conversation before. We're a team. We have each other's backs no matter what. "Don't fight me on this, Tiff. This is what we do, remember?"

I know she gets it when she gives me a small smile and nods. When she finally walks out of the room, I turn back to glare and Santos. I hope he can feel the anger radiating from me. I feel like it's coming off of me in waves.

"Is there a reason you think it's okay to tear into my wife like that? WAGs are off-limits."

Santos snorts a laugh, which infuriates me even more. "Just because you've been married for like three minutes doesn't make her a WAG in my book." He takes a swig of his beer and leans against the counter, looking like he doesn't have a care in the world. Like I won't do anything about this. But he's wrong.

I told my dad and my coach months ago, if it comes down to Tiffany or soccer, Tiffany will always be my choice. The moment I realized the truth of that statement, I felt free. Free to care for my wife and always put her first, no matter the consequence.

"I don't give a shit what your book says. You ever disrespect my wife like that again, and it'll come out of your face."

"Are you threatening me?"

"Damn right I am. I don't give a shit if you feel guilty about your marriage going south. That had nothing to do with her, and you're not going to try to project your feelings onto her, got it?"

He scoffs again. "Nothing to do with her? You realize she was there, right? You realize I was fucking *your wife*," he sneers, "on a regular basis, right?"

I step forward, and he immediately straightens. Finally, he understands that I have no concerns about defending her. None at all. Consequences be damned. And it's time I set him straight. "I know exactly what she used to do. I also know, instead of trying to throw all the blame for her actions onto other people, she tried to make amends. She didn't go to Mariana to give her all the details. Mariana went to her. Mariana already *knew,* Santos. She fucking knew you were cheating on her. She needed confirmation, so she could leave your sorry ass."

He narrows his eyes at me, but I'm not done.

"Let me ask you a question… the night Mariana left you, who were you fucking that night? It wasn't Tiffany, was it?"

He keeps getting more and more angry. His face is brighter red than I've seen, even after an hour of sprints. But this shit needs to end, and it needs to end now.

"I know because Tiffany was already done with that life by then," I remind him. "She did nothing wrong by answering Mariana's questions. In fact, those were the first honest answers Mariana actually got, because you sure as hell weren't telling her the truth. You need to take a good look at the role you played in *your* marriage before you spout shit in anyone else's direction. While you've been sitting around feeling sorry for yourself, Tiffany has been trying to make things right and gave Mariana the one thing in that conversation you hadn't given her… respect."

I turn to leave, my piece having been said. When I reach the door, though, I realize I have to make one more thing clear.

"One last thing." Turning back around, I glare at him. "I'm not a rookie anymore, and I'm not afraid of you. You ever speak about my wife like that again, whether she's in earshot or not, and I'll bash your fucking face in."

I storm into the living area and all eyes swing to mine. "Let's go." I grab Tiffany's hand, but she resists.

"Wait, wait, wait," she says, pulling out of grasp. "Are you not staying for poker night?"

"No way in hell can I be in the same room with that man right now," I spit out. "Sorry, Daniel. I know this is your last hurrah."

He waves me off as he passes out chips. "I get it, man. I'm just glad you didn't get blood in my kitchen. It's a bitch to disinfect."

"We still need to take these boxes to Quincy," Tiffany reminds me. "Even if I don't stay, she still needs them, and the baby needs this thingy." She waves the washcloth in my face.

I close my eyes and take a calming breath. "Fine. We'll drop them off."

She gives me a smile and whispers a quiet, "Thank you." I just nod and grab everything we're taking with us.

"Daniel," Tiffany calls out. She doesn't say anything until he looks up at her. "Don't say anything to Santos, okay? Let it go. I'm fine. He's just hurting."

Daniel considers for a few second, then nods once, and turns back to the game. As we walk out the door, I barely hear someone say, "See Christian? If you pulled your head out of your ass, you wouldn't have missed out on snatching up a good woman like her."

Tiffany chuckles at the exchange, but I'm still too riled up to find any humor in it. "Rowen," she calls out. I'm several feet ahead of her. "Rowen, stop," she calls again when I don't respond.

I ignore her, instead taking the time to situate the boxes in the back of the car and slamming the trunk. When I'm finally done, she's leaning against the car door, arms and legs crossed.

I stalk over and stand in front of her, hands on my hips.

"You okay now?" she asks but doesn't move.

"No."

"You gonna let him get to you every time he talks trash?"

"Maybe."

"You need to let it go."

I shake my head and run my hands through my hair in agitation, beanie forgotten at home. "How can you say that? He was in your face, screaming at you."

"I know. But he wasn't gonna hurt me."

"Physically. Emotionally is another story. He has no right to say those things to you."

"I agree. But Rowen, he is grieving right now."

"That is no excuse…"

"It's not an excuse. But it's a reason to give him a little bit of grace right now." She pushes off the car and puts her hands on my shoulders. "Babe, you saw the way he used to look at Mariana. He loves her so, so much."

"Then he should have kept his dick in his pants," I grumble.

"I agree. But he didn't, and he lost his entire family because of it." I shake my head at the absurdity of her defending the guy who just called her a whore, but she refuses to lose eye contact with me. "Look, I've forgiven myself and made amends the best I can. And you know how long and hard that process was. Multiply that guilt by a million, add in some children, and you have a really, really depressed guy." I look at the ground, not wanting to hear her justify his actions. "Think about it. If you had cheated on me—"

My eyes snap up to hers. "Never gonna happen—"

"—and I left, how would you feel? Your mistake wouldn't take the pain away, right?"

I put my hands back on my hips and blow out a breath. Fucking hell. She's right, and I hate that. "It still doesn't make it right…"

"I know. But part of the reason you're defending me is because you think he hurt me. Rowen, he didn't." I look at her skeptically. "No, really. He shocked me because I wasn't expecting it. But he didn't hurt me. I know where his anger is coming from. And I don't want you to have problems working with him over something that doesn't affect me at all."

Looking in her eyes, I try to assess if she's telling me the truth. Her face looks relaxed. There's a small smile on her lips. No tears in her eyes. She isn't lying about how she feels.

"I don't get you sometimes." Resting our foreheads together, I grab her around the waist and pull her to me.

"You're not supposed to. You're just supposed to tell me I'm right."

That gets a half smile from me. "I'm not telling you you're right about this. But I can respect that you don't want this to be a bigger deal than it has to be."

"Good enough." She kisses me softly and pulls away. "Come on. Let's get this stuff to Quincy so we can go home and get back in our honeymoon bubble."

I smile and agree, because what else am I going to do? Besides, that's where I'd wanted to be all along.

CHAPTER 3

Tiffany

The door clicks when it closes behind me as I walk into the newsroom. I'm immediately greeted by the sounds of the police scanners at the assignments desk, quietly squawking with whatever chatter emergency crews are talking about today.

Rowen and I took a few extra days off work when we got back from Fiji so we could settle into our new routine as husband and wife. And settle we did. After a lot of consideration, Rowen ended up moving into my apartment with me.

Although we liked the idea of living in the more secluded area of Rowen's garage apartment, moving to mine won out. Not because it's bigger and newer, but because it's closer to my job, which means it's less of a drive when I get off work in the middle of the night. Rowen also likes that since it's a big complex, there are more people around at all hours. He said he'll feel more comfortable about leaving me at home when he goes on the road.

Not that I haven't lived on my own for years, but he was raised to be chivalrous and protective. And boy does he take the idea of "protecting" me very, very seriously. I'm sure that would irritate a lot of women, but I find it to be amazing. He's always talking about how we're a team and we protect each other, so I have no complaints.

Now that we've been back into our daily routine for a couple of weeks, you'd think I wouldn't be excited about going into work again. Not today. I've been waiting for this particular day for weeks.

"What's up, Caleb?"

He barely looks at me when I drop my bags and grab the papers out of my mailbox. "If one more person calls out today, I'm going to lose my shit."

Sorting through my mail, I find mostly trash. What I need are story ideas for the rest of the week. With a sigh, I toss the trash in the recycle bin. "How many are out today?"

"Three photogs, two reporters, and one anchor. And I haven't even called production yet. I have no idea if they're missing people."

"Yikes." I lean against the desk. "That stomach bug again?"

"It's never ending. Just keeps making the rounds."

"I'm sorry. That sucks."

"Not just for me. Um… I have bad news."

My eyes widen. "No. Please don't say it."

"I'm sorry Tiffany. I don't have enough photogs to get the news covered."

"So you have to pull mine? From the one game we've

been looking forward to all year?"

Realistically, this happens all the time. If we're short-staffed or there is an overwhelming amount of local news, the sports photographer can be shifted over to the news department for the night. Normally, I don't complain. It's just part of the territory. It also goes both ways. When the Super Bowl was in Houston, news photographers worked in our department for a couple of days. Today though, this is the worst possible timing.

"I just don't know how else to make it work." He has the nerve to look sheepish, knowing he's just broken my sports-loving heart.

"But it's the Cowboys, Caleb," I plead. "The Cowboys never come to Houston."

"I know, and if there was any other way to make this work, I would do it."

Crossing my arms over my chest, I think of a plan. There's got to be a way to shuffle things around so everyone can get what they need.

I clear my throat. "Really, I don't need video of the entire game. We can get that from the feeds anyway."

"Tiff…" Caleb knows I'm not going to let this go without a fight.

"What I want is the last quarter and post-game interviews."

"Tiffany, what are you doing?"

I quirk an eyebrow at him. If I can just get him engaged, I might get what I want. "I think I know how this can work for both of us."

"All right, let's hear it." He's still looking at his monitors. That means he already doesn't think my idea will work. I'm going to have to work hard for this one.

"Let me put in a call to Jason Hart's manager. Tell him we want a post-game interview with him. It can be done in the locker room, or whatever. Doesn't have to be a sit-down type thing. We tell them we want to ask a few questions about his foundation, Hart to Heart."

"Uh huh."

He's not biting yet. Time to make it worth his while. "In the meantime, whichever anchor you have can start calling MD Anderson and see if they have the numbers of bone marrow matches from before Jason started the foundation until now. See if the numbers have increased."

He turns to look at me, eyes narrowed. "You have my attention now."

I smile at him. "I knew I would. Anyway, maybe the PR director at the cancer center knows a story or two about someone who waited for years to get a match but was unsuccessful until after all those bone marrow drives at the stadiums. Maybe the match was found because of that drive."

"I wonder if they could set it up where we could interview one of the survivors and their donor," Caleb offers, and I know I've got him.

"You read my mind. We could also share those stories with Jason and get his reaction to his foundation's hard work. In the meantime, I get my fourth quarter footage…"

"And I get an anchor package since I'm short on reporters…"

"Win-win."

"I'm going to need footage of the bone marrow drive when it was here. You think you can go through the archives and pull the b-roll for me?"

I hate going through the archives. But in this case, I'll do what it takes as long as I get the footage I want. "Absolutely.

I'll do it right now."

Caleb turns back to his computer screen. "Nice working with you, as always, Tiffany."

"Glad to be of service." Picking up my bags and the little bit of usable mail, I head toward the stairwell. "I'm gonna be upstairs now, away from the cesspool of germs."

"You know you just jinxed yourself," he calls after me.

"Took my Airborne this morning," I yell back with a laugh.

Okay that's a lie. But Caleb doesn't need to know that. It's too much fun getting a rise out of him. When I get to the sports office, Steve is already there.

"What are you doing here early?" I toss my bags on my desk and plop down in my chair.

"Wanted to make sure everything was set to go for the Cowboys game," he grumbles.

I don't like his tone. "And that put you in a bad mood?"

"No. Finding out today of all days our photog has been moved to news put me in a bad mood."

"Don't worry about it. Caleb and I got it worked out."

His looks at me and blinks, obviously not believing me. "What does that mean?"

I shrug. "Oh, ya know. We get fourth quarter footage and post-game interviews."

"How did you pull that off? Did you use your womanly charms against the defenseless Caleb?"

"What? Defenseless Caleb? What the fuck are you talking about?"

Steve clasps his hands behind his head. "That boy has had a crush on you since the first day of your internship."

I roll my eyes. "He has not. Give me a little credit. I came up with a good idea on how we can work together."

"Which is?"

"I'm calling Jason Hart's manager to set up a post-game interview asking about his foundation. And right now, someone downstairs is calling the cancer center to compare bone marrow numbers from before and after the drive at the stadium."

Steve nods his head once. "Wow. Nailed it. How come I didn't think of that?"

"My guess is, when you found out there was a switch-a-roo, you stomped off like a child, pouting instead of thinking it through."

"Ah, Tiffany, you know me well."

I spend several minutes booting up everything I'm going to need for the day, including digging through the archives.

For the most part, Steve and I work in silence, which isn't unusual. It's like the calm before the storm of multiple games on at once. It can get loud in here during peak hours.

But for now, the only conversation is when I call Hart's manager, Adam, and get everything set up. He's surprisingly pleasant about me calling last minute. But I guess Hart to Heart Foundation is important to them, since it was started when Jason's own son was fighting leukemia.

Going through the archives, I pull all the b-roll we're going to need for both the news and the sports story. It's above and beyond my job description, but everything about putting together a newscast is a team effort, so there's no reason to complain.

"Holy shit," Steve says behind me.

"What?" I'm only half listening, as I watch old video to make sure it's what we need.

"What do you think of New York?"

"New York the city? Or New York the state?"

"New York the market."

I freeze and look over at him. "As in the number one television market in the country?"

He nods.

"What about it?"

"News One has an associate sports producer position open."

My eyes widen. New York City is the largest local television market in the country because it has the largest demographic. It is quite literally the top of the local news food chain and because of that, almost never has open positions. No one leaves New York unless they go to a national network or die. And even then, it's not often. For a position to be open is huge, huge news.

"Don't you have family in New York?"

Steve nods slowly. "My wife does. She's always wanted to move closer to her family."

"Then I think you should go for it. You've gone as far as you can in this market. It would be a huge step up for you."

He nods thoughtfully and then quickly smiles, like the whole thing is ridiculous. "It's just a pipe dream anyway. Everyone knows how hard it is to get in there." He's right. There are going to thousands of applicants. He knows it. I know it. Everyone who works in the biz knows it.

"Yeah, but what a nice pipe dream."

I get back to my research but watch him out of the corner of my eye. He's downplaying his excitement, but I know he wants that job. And I want him to have it. Not just for him but for me.

Steve is the best boss, and I won't be happy to see him go. But if he leaves, that means *his* position will need to be filled. And maybe if we're lucky, both our dreams will come true.

CHAPTER 4

Rowen

Pepto. Soup. Crackers. Sprite. Deodorant.... What else?

I can't remember. Tiffany told me to make list this morning when I told her I was going to the store after practice. Did I listen? No. So now I'm wandering around Walmart, which I already hate, trying to remember what she told me to get.

I look in my cart and run down my mental list again.

Pepto. Soup. Crackers. Sprite.... Got all that.

Turning down the aisle, I dodge a child who runs in front of my cart. That right there is why I'm okay with not having any kids right now, despite the inevitable questions from everyone asking why Tiffany and I eloped. I can't remember everything on my shopping list. How would I be able to keep up with a kid? I love Tiffany, and when the time is right, it'll happen. But I'm good with waiting for a while.

Pepto. Soup. Crackers. Sprite… ooh! A three pack of my favorite deodorant is on sale! I snag that sucker and toss it in the cart. Athletes go through a shit ton of hygiene products. We have to unless we want to smell like funky BO all the time, which I don't.

Finally giving up, I grab my phone and dial. Tiffany picks up on the second ring and before I can even say anything, she proves why she's my better half.

"Maxi pads and tampons. I need maxi pads and tampons."

"How did you know that's why I was calling?" I start looking up and down the aisle to see if I'm anywhere close to the lady Band-Aid section.

"Because you didn't write it down this morning when I told you to."

"I was practicing my short-term memory."

"And how's that working out for you?" she jokes.

"Not bad, actually. I found a three-pack of deodorant on sale while I was wandering around, trying to figure it out."

"That absolutely makes up for not writing out a list." Her throaty laugh throws my libido in high gear again. It doesn't matter that she's been sick for damn near a week. I still want her with an intensity I can't even describe. It could be because I'm still new at this whole sex thing, but it's more likely because we have such a strong connection, not just physically. She's my best friend. I like being with her more than anyone else in the world.

"All right, all right. I'll write it down next time. You can stop making fun. Now where am I going to find these things?"

"Are you still in the deodorant aisle?"

"Yep."

"Two aisles down when you head toward the exit."

I make my way around more children and an employee stocking the shaving cream. Because the middle of the day is a great time to stock shelves. "How are you feeling anyway?"

"Well I haven't thrown up in the last, oh, three hours. This stomach bug is brutal. No wonder so many people called out of work."

"And now you have your monthly friend, so that's even better."

"No, I don't," she says with a grunt. I assume she's shifting around on the couch, which is where I left her this morning. "I just happened to look under the cabinet today when I was praying to the porcelain god and realized I was almost out."

"What? You're making me suffer this humiliation for something you don't even need yet?"

"First, you'd much rather me have them readily available for when I need them, than have to clean up that mess. Just trust me."

I grimace at the thought.

"Second, this shows everyone around you that you're man enough to have a good woman by your side."

I chuckle. "I'll take your word on all that."

"Are you there yet?" she asks impatiently.

"No. Still dodging random obstacles in my way," I say as a third kid runs in front of me. Seriously, I play less defense on the soccer field than I do here.

"So Steve called."

"Your boss, Steve?"

"Yep."

"I hope he's not giving you shit for calling out…"

"No, no. Not at all. Adam, Jason Hart's manager called."

My eyebrows shoot up in interest. "And?"

"And they want permission to use my story from a couple weeks ago as part of their marketing for his foundation."

"That's great, babe!" I congratulate. "That's huge for your résumé."

"I know. I'll have ESPN calling me before you know it."

I can hear the smile in her voice. Her biggest dream is to produce sports shows for that channel. Watching her make small steps the right direction is fun to see.

"I'm really proud of you."

"Thanks. Are you there yet?"

"Yep. I'm here, and no small children have been run over. What am I looking for?"

"Look on your left. You see all the condoms and lube and stuff?"

"Should I be worried that you can visualize the birth control aisle at Walmart?" I rib.

"Shut up, Rookie. I have to hit that aisle once a month, remember? Look just to the right of those items, and you'll see the tampons."

My eyes widen. "There are a lot of boxes."

"I know. You're looking for a pink box. It has a giant P on it..."

"Got it!" I grab the box feeling victorious and read it off to her. "Playtex Sport, Regular size, plastic applicator... Babe... are you sure this is what you want?"

"Nicely done," she praises. "That's exactly it. Toss that puppy in the cart."

"Tiff, are these the inside ones or outside ones?"

"What?"

I lower my voice hoping no one around hears me. "Do these go inside you or stay outside on your underwear?"

"Seriously? You're twenty-four years old. How do you

not know which ones these are?”

“Really?” I contend. “You were there. Up until a few weeks ago, there wasn’t a whole lot of vagina talk in my world.”

She laughs again. “Touché. Those are the inside ones.”

This makes me concerned. “Babe. That doesn’t seem safe. To have plastic inside you all day?”

She howls with laugher this time. I can practically hear the tears running down her face.

“I don’t understand what’s funny about me being concerned for your safety.”

“I love you, Rowen,” she says as she tries really hard to pull herself together. “But that’s just the applicator.”

“Yeah, but it goes inside you.”

“It doesn’t stay there.”

“It doesn’t?” I rub my face. “I’m confused.”

“When you get home, I’ll give you tampon 101 and explain it.”

“Okay, I give up.” I throw the box in the cart, giving up the fight. “What am I looking for now?”

“Turn around and look on the opposite side of the aisle.”

Holy. Shit. There are so many boxes. Everything from panty looking diapers to teeny tiny things folded in half.

“Babe.”

I know she hears how overwhelmed I am. “Relax. I know it’s a lot to take in. You’re looking for a green box.”

“Green box. Okay. Looking for a green box.” I start searching the shelves for anything that looks green.

“Inside the green box is a bunch of yellow packages.”

“I have to open up all the green boxes?”

“No, babe. You can see the yellow packages through the plastic window on the box.”

That makes more sense. "Okay. Green box. Yellow packages."

"It's called Always Infinity."

"I'm still looking for a green box. I can't see what it's called…" Suddenly, it's in my hand. A woman, probably in her early forties, pats me on the arm.

"Pretty sure this is what she's asking you for," she says with a smile.

"Let me double check. Babe, someone just handed me a box. It's green, I can see yellow packages inside. It's called Always Infinity, size… uh… regular? Is that right?"

"That's exactly it!"

"Thank you!" I tell the woman, as she smiles and begins to walk away.

"You're welcome. You aren't the first man I've had to help on this aisle, and you won't be the last."

Tiffany giggles. "She's got that right."

"Yeah, yeah. That's everything on the list, right?"

"What do you have?"

I look back in the cart because, once again, I forgot. I really need to make a list. "Soup, crackers, Sprite, Pepto, my three-pack of on-sale deodorant…"

She snorts a laugh.

"And all your woman things."

"You did good, Rookie. Are you headed home now?"

The area widens as I turn the cart onto the main aisle. It feels much less claustrophobic now that I'm not packed in with so many other people all looking for the same thing. I need to get out of here. "Yeah. I've got a couple hours until I have to get back."

"How's it going with Santos?" she asks gently. Santos is a tough topic for Tiffany and me. I think she gives him too much leeway on being a dick. She thinks I don't give him enough. We could agree to disagree because in different ways, we're both right. But working with him every day makes it tough to let it go. And working with him every day means I can tell things aren't getting better with him.

"I don't know, Tiffany. I kind of feel bad for the guy. He hasn't said anything or gotten in my face again. But he's just… off."

"Well, his whole life is in upheaval."

"I know. That's why I didn't beat his ass that night at poker. You were right, and I'm trying to give him breathing room. And he wants to do drills all the time now, so at least I'm getting extra practice with my corner shot. As long as he's not taking pot-shots at you, I'm okay with just letting him be. It just kind of sucks."

"Has he mentioned anything about Mariana or the kids?"

"Nope. He stays really tight-lipped." I get in the back of a very long check-out line. We're at least ten deep, but of course it's the only lane open. "But we don't really run in the same circle, anyway. I think he's kind of lost."

"I wish I could do something for him. As much as he's a dick to me now, he really was kind to me for a long time."

I bristle. Tiffany's sexual history doesn't really affect me anymore, but every once in a while, it's still bothersome that I have to see her former sex partners every day. I know we're married and the past doesn't really matter. But no man wants to think about their woman being with someone else.

"I'm sorry," she says quietly, picking up on my mood change. "I didn't mean to bring it up."

"No, babe. Don't ever feel sorry for feeling bad for someone. Your heart is what I love about you the most."

"You're sweet."

"Sweet enough to get a little action when I get there?" The woman in front of me turns around and glares at me. I shrug and pretend I don't care, even though I feel my face flaming.

"Maybe," Tiffany says coyly. "Um… maybe not…" She doesn't sound so coy anymore. "Oh shit, I gotta go babe. Fuck, I thought this was over…"

She must miss the "end call" button because I hear her take off running and what I assume is the bathroom door slam. I disconnect as the line slowly inches forward and stops.

If I can only get out of here, I'll be able to get the supplies home to my sick wife.

CHAPTER 5

The pop of a comb on my head jars me awake.

"Ow!" I cry. "What'd you do that for?"

"You keep falling asleep in my chair," Quincy quips. "Makes it impossible to get this color done right if your head keeps bobbing."

"Sorry. I don't know what my problem is," I admit. "I can't seem to get enough sleep lately."

"It's all those late-night romps with your lover," Geni sing-songs.

"Geni! You have a client!" Quincy admonishes.

"So?" She holds up her first finger for us to give her a minute. "John," she says to the client sitting in her chair. "Are you even listening to what I say?"

"Nope." He doesn't look up from his phone. "I've got

three daughters and a wife. I know how to tune you guys out."

Geni makes an "I told you so" gesture. "Anyway, like I was saying. You'll probably feel better once you get out of this newlywed phase."

"Please," I argue. "I've been so sick lately, there has been no newlywed phase."

"You're gonna try to convince me you aren't having sex at least once every night."

I playfully pretend to avoid the question, looking around the room until she huffs, and I give. "Okay fine. I won't try to convince you of that."

"I knew it!" Geni says, as she brushes the cut hairs off John's shoulders. "I knew you had bags under your eyes for a reason. Come on, John, let's get you checked out."

John takes a minute to look at his hair in the mirror before following her to the front desk, untraumatized by our conversation.

"Sorry about her," Quincy says quietly.

"Quincy, don't be sorry. Geni and I get along just fine. Who would have thunk, right?"

"You guys have come a long way." She folds another foil on my head. "How are you feeling anyway?"

"Better, I guess. This stomach bug is the worst, but I have to go back to work today. I've been off for too long."

"Hmm."

I know better than to think her response doesn't have more substance behind it than she's letting on. "What? What is that hmm for?"

"Oh nothing."

"Quincy…"

"I just…" She hems and haws around the conversation for a few minutes until she finally can't hold it in anymore.

"Okay, I'm just gonna say it. Are you pregnant?"

"What? No." I shake my head vehemently.

"Tiffany, you can't stay awake. You've had the stomach bug for a week now. When was your last period?"

"It was…" I pause, because I honestly don't remember. She quirks an eyebrow at me. "Don't look at me like that. I think it was the week of Thanksgiving."

"You think?"

"I think because I know I was supposed to have it while Steve was out of town and I took over for him. But I have no recollection because I didn't take many bathroom breaks while he was gone. I was too busy, so I don't remember. But I don't remember *not* having it either."

"That means you think you had it?"

"Of course. I have no reason to question it. I had Rowen buy what he calls lady Band-Aids the other day because I had run out."

She giggles. "Daniel hates it when I send him to buy tampons."

I smile conspiratorially. "It's fun, though, isn't it?"

"What's fun?" Geni asks, as she plops down in her chair.

"Making the guys buy maxi pads."

"Erik flat out refuses." She grabs a magazine off her counter and flips through it. "We actually had our first fight over it. I had to stuff the undies with toilet paper and go buy them myself."

"Are you serious?" Quincy crinkles her nose in disgust. "I would kill Daniel if he did that to me!"

Geni shrugs. "I was pissed when it happened. But Erik's quirky. We all know that. The next night he took me out for a steak dinner to make up for it."

We chat a little more about the guys and baby Chance and

the latest team gossip. It's weird to think that a year or so ago, Quincy and I had a rocky relationship, and Geni and I couldn't stand each other. I wouldn't call us besties now or anything. But it's kind of nice having some female friends that I see outside of soccer. It's a bonus that they ended up being "couple" friends.

Quincy clears her throat. "So… I have news."

Geni slams the magazine shut and leans forward. "Do tell. I love it when you have news."

Quincy shoots her an annoyed look. "Why are you acting like I'm announcing the next Oscar nominees?"

"Because you *are* making an announcement. You don't ever clear your throat and say, 'I have news' unless it's really exciting and gossipy. Spill."

Quincy rolls her eyes and turns to look at me in the mirror. "It's being announced to the team today. In fact, it probably already was."

"What was? What was?" Geni bounces in her seat.

"You are a little too excited about this," I judge.

"Oh, you just wait," Geni says. "I have known this one for a very long time. I can tell when it's going to be juicy." She waves towards Quincy. "Continue."

"I need to rethink this friendship," Quincy mumbles, taking another swipe of the brush in the color and bringing it to my head. "Okay, it's being announced today, but… Nate Funderling's been traded."

I gasp.

"No!" Geni cries out, hand over her mouth. "Are you sure?"

"Yep. It's a done deal."

"To where?" Geni demands. "Please tell me it's somewhere terrible."

"Vancouver, I think? Maybe Montreal. I can't remember. Somewhere in Canada."

Geni throws her head back and begins cracking up.

"That is the exact opposite of the weather here," I say with a smile on my face. "I bet Jessica is pissed."

There is no love lost between Nate's wife, Jessica Funderling, and me. She attacked me in the family box during a game last year when she was drunk. It bruised my ego more than anything, but it got her banned from attending events on the team's dime again. Knowing she's leaving doesn't make me upset at all.

"Poor Jessica," Geni spouts with a sarcastic pout. "No more too-short mini-skirts, halter tops, and strappy sandals for her. Just snow suits and giant hoods over her head."

"Don't forget the ski masks and scarves," I chime in.

"I bet she is shitting her pants right now," Geni continues.

"Guys," Quincy cuts in, "just in case it hasn't been announced yet, don't say anything. You know Daniel is supposed to keep everything confidential. This just feels way more… personally victorious in some ways."

"You won't hear a word from me," I say.

"Who am I gonna tell?" Geni asks with a shrug. "Erik doesn't even like sports unless it's football. He barely knows Daniel's name, and his son lives with him."

Quincy titters because it's true. As nice as Erik is, he just doesn't get it. His interest in baby Chance seems to be more about his mother's desire to be a grandmother than him being a father. I don't see what attracts Geni to him, but hey… no one could figure out what Rowen saw in me, so to each his own, I suppose.

"Done." Quincy drops her brush back in the bowl and wipes her hands with a towel. "Let's get you to the dryers. I can't wait to see what these highlights are going to look like on you."

I grab my phone and get situated under the dryers. Once I'm settled, Quincy takes off to work on another client while my color processes.

What I'd never admit to her is that she's not the first to wonder if I'm pregnant. I've been thinking about it for a few days now. I know I was supposed to start the week of Thanksgiving, but I can't remember if I did or not. I had supplies with me, but the only ones still in my bag are squished at the bottom. It's impossible to tell if they've been there for a few weeks or a few months.

I scroll through the overnight sports scores, keeping my mind off the potential problem at hand, when a text comes through. It's my husband. Just calling him that in my head automatically makes me smile.

Rowen: *I have news.*

Me: *Funderling's been traded?*

Rowen: *How did you know?*

Me: *You forget I have fantastic journalism skills.*

Rowen: *Journalism skills or a hair appointment with Quincy?*

Me: *You say that like they're mutually exclusive.*

Rowen: *Aren't they?*

Me: *... a good journalist never reveals her sources.*

Rowen: *Understood. I figured you'd like to hear that news.*

Me: *Can't say it makes me unhappy. So it's for sure now? I can actually report this tonight?*

Rowen: *I guess. Big wigs know better than to tell a bunch of old bitties in the locker room anything they don't want getting out.*

Me: *You guys are a bunch of gossip queens. Remind me never to tell you anything in confidence.*

Rowen: *This is why I keep my mouth shut. I'd much rather know everything than be known by everyone.*

Rowen: *How are you feeling, anyway?*

Scared. But I can't tell him. Not yet.

Me: *Not fantastic, but better. I haven't thrown up yet today.*

Rowen: *I really think you should take the day off.*

Me: *No way. I was off for five days already. We JUST got back from vacation. I can't afford to take any more time. As long as I don't have a fever. I'm fine.*

Rowen: *Fine but be careful. I'll be waiting for you when you get home.*

Me: *I know you will. I love you, babe. Don't forget to tell the trainers to massage that right calf of yours. You don't want it cramping up again. Especially while you're tapping this ass.*

Rowen: *Yes, ma'am! P.S. I love it when you're bossy. Love you.*

Me: *;) Love you too.*

I scroll through more sports stories, getting my brain ready for work. The final score of last night's Cowboys game reminds me to check the *Hart to Heart* website.

It pulls up fast and is easy to navigate. Very quickly, I find what I'm looking for—my report from two weeks ago. I can feel how wide I'm smiling, and I don't care if it looks cheesy. My story, my report, is on Jason Hart's website. A website that gets millions of clicks every year, and I have a credit at the end of the report.

That story would never have happened if I hadn't made a deal with Caleb. I'm really proud of myself. This is what I love. It's what I'm good at. And it paid off in a big way this time.

The dryer suddenly cuts out. "You ready?" Quincy asks as she shuts off the dryer and inspects the color underneath the foils.

I click off the site. "Sure. Let's go."

Before I know it, she's washed my hair, which almost put me to sleep, combed through my hair, which almost put me to sleep, and has started cutting my hair, which has almost put me to sleep.

"Ow!" I cry, the sting of the comb as it slaps my head jarring me again. "Why the hell do you keep doing that?"

"Because you fell asleep again," Quincy retorts. "I can't very well cut your hair straight if your head keeps moving."

"Sorry," I mumble. "I didn't realize I dozed off again."

"I don't know how you're going to stay awake at work tonight." She grabs her phone and reads a text.

"No one washes my hair and rubs my head at work."

"True." She begins typing with her thumbs. "Do you want anything from Jason's Deli? Geni's offering. She ran out to get food."

I scrunch my nose and shake my head. "No way. Just the thought of lunch meat makes me want to throw up again." Quincy pauses her texting to look up at me. I roll my eyes. "Don't even say it."

"I won't say it." She tosses the phone down and picks up her scissors. "But promise me you'll start watching for your period."

"I will, but Quincy, I've been on the shot for a long time, and I've never had a problem before. This is just a coincidence."

"I know. But Rowen waited to be sexually active for a long time. There's no telling how strong his swimmers are, being dormant for so many years."

That one makes me chuckle. It would totally be my luck that Rowen has super strong swimmers that can get past even the heaviest of birth control.

"How about this?" I offer. "If I don't get my period by Monday, I'll go out and waste a bunch of money buying a test that will say I'm *not* pregnant, okay?"

"Okay," she says finally appeased. "And you'll let me know on Monday."

"I will let you know on Monday."

I'm lying. I know I am. I will never admit that I already had my suspicions, but I was trying to ignore them. Now that Quincy has forced me to really think about it, I'm not waiting until Monday to buy a test. I'm doing it on my way to work.

CHAPTER

6

Rowen

Rubbing my face, I look around the room trying to get my bearings straight. Something woke me up and, judging by the sound of Tiffany coming around the corner, I assume it was her closing the front door.

"Hey, babe," I say, as I sit up, leaning against the arm of the couch. "How was work?"

She drops her bag next to the couch, shoes already gone. She's so tiny compared to me that she's able to squeeze herself between my legs and the back of the couch, and I'm still not close to falling off the edge. Somehow, her feet end up on my lap, so I begin digging my thumb into her arches.

She groans in pleasure. "How did you know I was going to need my feet rubbed tonight?"

"Lucky guess," I shrug. "Your hair looks nice."

"Thanks. Quincy added highlights."

"They look good. How was work?"

"Same as always. I take it you didn't watch the show?"

I flinch. When she's at work, I try to watch the sports segment. She watches all my games, why wouldn't I support her the same way? "I'm sorry, babe. I fell asleep at some point. These two-a-days are killing me."

"You're an old man, now, Rookie. Trying to keep up with those whipper-snappers."

"Or, I'm trying to keep up with my wife's insatiable sexual appetite, and I'm not getting enough sleep."

A weird look crosses her face. I can't quite figure out what it is, but after this long together, I know she's got something on her mind. Something big.

"Yeah. That's probably it." She turns to face the TV, attention diverted to the magical fairy covered in blood on the screen. "What are you watching, anyway?"

"*FaceOff*. Have you ever seen it?"

She shakes her head but doesn't look at me.

"It's really cool. It's this competition show on Syfy where all these prosthetic makeup artists and designers create new characters every week. They're really good. I just watched one of the models do a back flip in front of the judges, while in full costume. It's unreal."

We watch for a little bit in silence, me still massaging her feet.

"What do they win?" she asks, as the show takes a commercial break.

"I don't know yet," I admit. "I haven't gotten through the first season."

"How many seasons are there?"

"Like eighteen or something."

"Eighteen?" She guffaws. "You're never gonna see my show again."

I love watching her laugh. She has the best smile. "I will too. I might turn this right back on as soon as the sports segment is over."

She goes back to watching the show, and I go back to watching her. She's looking at the television, but I can tell she's not really seeing it. Her eyes are too glazed, and she's worrying her lip. Something is definitely up.

I nudge her with my foot. "Hey." She ignores me, so I try again. "Hey. What's going on with you."

She takes a deep breath and drops her head to the back of the couch. "We're just so young, ya know?"

I cock my head. That's a really strange way to start a conversation. But she's not done.

"And we have all these plans. What if you get traded out of state? What if I get picked up nationally?"

Now my heart is pounding. Something very wrong, and she's starting to freak me out.

"There are just so many unknowns…"

Quickly, I move from the couch to the coffee table in front of her, grabbing her hands. "Tiff…" I try to interrupt, but she keeps babbling.

"This is not what we signed up for. Not what we wanted…"

"Tiff…" I try again.

"I don't see how this is going to work…"

"Tiffany," I say forcefully. She finally looks at me, the crinkle between her brows a dead giveaway that whatever she's about to tell me is really bad. "Are we okay?"

She looks sad and scared. "I don't know."

My heart drops and my blood runs icy through my veins.

"Why?" I watch as she looks back and forth across my face, considering her next words carefully. After what feels like forever, she sighs, releases my hands and reaches down to dig through her bag.

When she straightens up, she puts a white stick in my hands. "I'm pregnant."

Leaning my elbow on my knee, I cover my mouth and stare at the two pink lines that just changed my life forever. I don't know whether to laugh or cry. All I know is I have a whole lot of mixed emotions.

"Yer pregnant."

Tiffany nods sadly, waiting for me to respond to the bomb she just dropped. "Say something," she pleads, putting her hand on my knee.

I clear my throat of the emotion before speaking. "I'm not sure what to say."

"I'm sorry, Rowen. I know this is terrible timing…"

My eyes whip up to hers. "Ye think I'm upset?"

"Aren't you?"

"Tiffany, I'm so excited, I can't find words to adequately express how I feel." Putting the test next to me, I pull her onto my lap, her legs straddling me. Instinctively, her arms go around my neck. "I know ye think we're too young and all that. But babe, it's not about what timing is good for us. It's about him."

"*Him*, huh?" She smiles, tears glistening in her eyes.

"Or *her*. My point is, there's a reason this baby is coming into the world unexpectedly. Our job is to raise him or *her* and guide him until he figures out the reason it has to be now."

Tiffany looks at me, her face more relaxed than it was just a few minutes ago. She leans in and when our lips connect, the frenzy begins. I love nothing more than kissing my wife. But now that I know she's carrying my child, my *child, our* child, I want nothing more than to be tangled up with her forever.

"Holy shit. I'm gonna be a Dadaí," I say reverently when we break apart to catch our breath. She rubs her hand down my cheek and scratches gently at my scruff.

"I love you, Rowen."

"I love you too." I look down at my hand that has somehow made its way down to her hip, my thumb caressing her still flat stomach. "And I love you too, *A Leanbh.*"

Reaching up, I kiss Tiffany again, this time slowly and with all the feelings running through me now. This moment right here is the single best moment of my life. Knowing that it will pale in comparison to what's coming in the next few months is surreal.

"Tiff," I break away again and pull back to look at her. "Um… can we do something?"

She quirks an eyebrow at me. "Is it something kinky?"

I smack her ass playfully and pick her up to drop her back on the couch. "Dirty girl. No. I wanna call my parents."

"What? You realize it's after midnight in Detroit, right?"

"You realize my mam would kill me if I didn't tell her right away, don't you?"

"Touché. But why call them when you can just Face-Time?"

"Good idea." I grab for my laptop on the end table and switch it on.

"I was being sarcastic."

"I know. But it was still a good idea." The computer whirs to life, and I begin pulling up the contact information. "Man, I wish I knew how to record FaceTime calls. I bet this is one I'm gonna want to watch again tomorrow."

I settle in next to Tiffany and she rests her head on my

shoulder, as the call goes through. Within seconds, my mother's face pops up on the screen, concern etched all over her face. She's obviously in bed, reading glasses on, the glow of the bedside lamp illuminating the screen.

"Rowen? Is everything okay?"

"Yeah, Mam." I can feel how big I'm grinning. She's liable to think I'm drunk if I smile any wider. "We just needed to talk to ye. Did I wake you up?"

"No, I'm just reading." She nudges my father, trying to rouse him awake. "You know what a night owl I am. Hi, Tiffany. Are you okay, dear?"

Tiffany nods and sits up a little straighter. "I am. Still a little sluggish, but better."

"Good." Mam nudges my dad a little harder. "Ryan, honey, wake up."

He grunts and shifts in bed but doesn't move other than that.

"Ryan!" She's full on pushing him now. Tiffany buries her face in the crook of my neck as she and I try hard not to laugh, but the scene is pretty humorous. Eventually Da rolls over and notices us.

"Rowen? What the fuck, *boyo*? Someone better be knocking on death's door, or I'm gonna lob ye one next time ye visit."

"Nice to see you too, Da." He grunts and sits up against the headboard, causing the sheet to fall down a little too much. Tiffany's hand claps over her eyes and I immediately try to cover up the screen. "Ah! Da! Cover yerself, man! My wife is right here!"

"Don't wake me up at the bewitching hour if ye don't want yer woman to get an eyeful," he retorts, crossing his arms over his broad chest.

I've gotta give it to my dad. He's still in fantastic shape for his age. I can only hope those genetics passed down to me.

"Well we need to talk to ye, and it couldn't wait."

"Is everything okay, Rowen?" my mam asks. "You sound upset."

I look at Tiffany and smile. "Not upset, Mam."

"Then what?"

Tiffany shrugs. "Don't look at me. It was your idea to call them in the middle of the night."

Taking a deep breath, I look back at the screen and hold up the pregnancy test for my parents to see. Mam gasps, her hand covering her mouth.

Da groans.

"What is that?" He squints his eyes to see better. "A pen?" The sheets rustle around as he starts to lie back down. "Ye wake me up from a sexy dream about your mam to show me some sort of fancy team swag?" Mam smacks his leg gently to get his attention, but he's too determined to get comfortable to notice. "Send me a box of em in the mail tomorrow. I'm going back to sleep."

Tiffany has given up the fight and is now holding her belly, side probably in stitches.

"Ryan." Mam is still smacking him, but it's getting less gentle as he ignores her. "Ryan! That's not a fancy pen! That's a pregnancy test!"

Tiffany waves her hands in front of her eyes and tries to get her breathing under control, so she can stop giggling. Tears are running down her face from laughing. I'm smiling so wide, I must look like a damn fool. And Da looks back over his shoulder, suddenly wide awake.

This. This right here is why I wish I knew how to record FaceTime calls. A stubborn Irish man's got nothing on a woman who just found out she's going to be a *Maimeó*.

It takes a few seconds for him to roll over. I'm still holding the test, but I've moved it a little closer to the camera where they can see. Da leans forward and squints. Mam is smiling and wiping tears off her cheeks behind him.

"Well, what the hell do the pink lines mean?" he asks, completely stumped as to what's happening.

And Tiffany loses it again. She's laughing so hard, she's not making a sound. I drop my head to my chest as my whole body feels like it's convulsing from this shitshow. Somehow, we end up leaning into each other as we just keep laughing… at my dad. At the ridiculousness of the situation. At the overwhelming joy we didn't even know was missing until now.

I can hear my mother in the background explaining what two pink lines means, but I'm not paying much attention. I'm too busy enjoying this moment.

Suddenly, the emotion begins to overwhelm me. I drop my head to my chest, squeezing the bridge of my nose and grasping for Tiffany. Our right hands intertwine, and she starts rubbing my back with her other hand. She just knows I'm going to crack soon.

I've never been so happy. So scared. So peaceful. So frantic. And it's all happening at once. It's overwhelming in the best way imaginable.

"Look at me, *Mack*," Da orders. I look up, expecting for him to poke fun at me for getting emotional. His words surprise me instead. "The proudest day of me life was when you were born. I cried like a *babaí* as soon as they put you in me arms. Ask yer mam. Having so much love for yer child… those are the manliest tears you can ever have."

I take a deep breath and rub my face. "I just can't believe I'm gonna be a Dadaí." More sniffing. More blinking tears away.

"Congrats, Mack. Ye make me proud."

Tiffany and my mom chat a while longer about her symptoms and what Mam's pregnancy with me was like. Before I know it, we've been talking for over an hour.

"*Mo grá*," Da says to my mam as I yawn. "We need to let them go te bed. Rowen may have gotten her knocked up, but that doesn't give him an excuse to not practice in the morn."

I chuckle, and my mam rolls her eyes. "All right, all right. I'm glad you let us know, though. I know I can't share it yet, but I can't wait to start shopping for baby clothes!"

Tiffany stiffens slightly, not enough for them to see, but enough for me to notice. "Why don't you wait a few more months, Denise? We've got lots of time."

"So you think," Mam responds. "It'll fly by before you know it."

We say our goodbyes and end the call, me taking Tiffany's hand in mine and kissing her palm. "You know she's going to start shopping tomorrow."

"I know." Tiff leans her head on my shoulder. "I'm really tired. Can we go to bed now?"

I stand up and pull her to her feet, pecking her on the lips. "Am I gonna get some tonight?"

She holds up her finger. "On one condition."

"What's that?"

Her hand drops to her stomach and she begins to rub. The look on her face tells me she's not tired anymore. She's playful. I like it. "We don't want to squish the baby. I need to be on top."

My eyes widen and my dick twitches. "Done."

She giggles as I drag her behind me, heading back into our bubble, now expanded by one.

59

CHAPTER

7

The gynecologist office is not my idea of a good time. But I'm pretty sure that's a given for anybody. The room is always too cold. The flimsy gowns are always too small. And there's no way to hide your butt crack from anyone who opens the door.

Plus, I hate the crinkly paper on the exam table. For whatever reason, the sound is like nails on a chalkboard to me. Thankfully, I'm sitting on one of those puppy pad things, so I don't feel the paper on my naked ass too.

Rowen, of course, is sitting in the one chair that fits in the room, the lucky bastard, while I sit as still as I can trying not to move the crinkly paper. It's making my back hurt, but I'll take the lesser of two evils.

"What's wrong?" he asks, long legs stretched out across the floor.

"Nothing. Why?"

"You look really nervous." I shoot him a puzzled look. "You're completely stiff."

"Oh. That. I'm trying not to make the paper move."

"Why?"

"I hate the way it sounds. It grates on my nerves and makes me want to stab my ear drums out."

He smiles in amusement. "That's some serious hate."

"I know. I'm trying not to breathe very hard, so it doesn't move."

Suddenly, he stands up and begins ripping the paper off the table.

"What are you doing?" I look around frantically, like someone is going to see him and kick us out.

"What does it look like?" He wads up the offending paper and tosses it in the trash. "There. Problem solved."

"You can't just do that, Rowen. What if, what if… I don't know, what if that was important or something."

"Babe. It's not going to hurt anything. They only use the paper to protect the tables from wear and tear."

"That's not true. It's for germ control."

He quirks an eyebrow at me. "You think paper so thin that it tears on contact is protecting you from germs?"

"I… well…" He makes a good point, actually. "How do you know this anyway?"

His cheeks immediately flush. "I just know."

Now I know he's lying. "No way. You're not getting off that easy. Seriously. How do you know?"

He sighs and shoots me a playful grin. "Fine. There was a contestant on FaceOff who happened to be a medical assistant by trade. It came up during one of their weird hospital-themed challenges."

"Ohmygod, that's funny," I giggle, trying really hard not to move the paper that's still under my butt, to no avail. I grimace when it crinkles again.

Rowen immediately stands up, takes the two steps to reach me and taps my leg. "Up." As soon as my naked feet hit the step, he snatches the paper, leaving the puppy pad in place. "Okay, you can sit," he says as he gooses my breast, making me shriek.

"Rowen!" I swat at him. He just laughs, the asshole. "Quit it!"

"Oh, give me a break. You're pregnant. Everyone in this office knows how that happened."

I roll my eyes and settle back onto the table, much more comfortable now that the damn paper is gone. My thoughts wander back to the previous conversation and I snort a laugh. "I still can't believe you got all your medical knowledge from the Syfy channel."

"Hey now. Don't make fun of me. It's making me well-rounded."

We settle back into our seats and back into our thoughts. It's still really surreal being in this room with my husband, getting ready to find out more information about our baby. A year ago, I never would have expected this. Hell, six months ago, we were just dating. But here we are.

I think about how this is going to work. How much I don't want my child to grow up in daycare. I did that. It wasn't because my mom had a choice. My dad ditched us long before I can remember.

I don't feel like she was never there for me. But I always thought my friends whose moms stayed home were so lucky.

I'd wondered what it would be like to go straight home from school and sit down at the table with a snack and tell my mom about my day before we went to gymnastics lessons or softball practice.

Then, as I got older and became a latchkey kid, I didn't mind being home alone. What teenager does? But I did always wonder what it would be like for my mom to make dinner for me instead of the other way around.

It wasn't a bad life. I don't feel like I missed out. It's just… not what I want for *my* child. And I don't know how to balance that with my passion for my job.

"Um… there's a party this weekend."

My eyes snap up to look at Rowen, who seems really uncomfortable bringing up this topic. "Okay. Are you wanting to go or something?"

He pulls his beanie off and runs his fingers through his hair. He doesn't wear the beanie very much anymore, unless he's trying hard to hide those flaming red locks. Today, with the news of the pregnancy being new and us not wanting to tell anyone yet, I'm guessing he's trying to be as incognito as possible.

"It's Funderling's going-away party."

I nod slowly in understanding. "Ah."

He scratches at his scruff, still acting very unsure of this conversation. "I really don't want to go. I don't even like the guy and I'm glad he's leaving. But…"

"You feel like you have to go for team unity purposes."

"Yes," he says in a rush. "We don't have to go. It's not a big deal."

"Yes, it is. I know how team politics go. You need to show up, play nice, and pretend to give a shit so on Monday, you're not the guy who didn't show."

"Yeah," he exhales, relieved that I understand why he's conflicted.

I stretch my back and think for a minute before saying, "I think we should both go."

"You do?" The amount of surprise on his face is almost comical.

"Look, I hate the idea of pretending to give a shit that they're moving to Canada or wherever, but it won't kill us to play nice for the sake of the team."

"I hate taking you back into that environment. After everything…"

"Rowen, stop," I interrupt. "Yes, it will be a little uncomfortable. But I'm assuming Daniel and Quincy will be there, right?"

One of his shoulder raises like he assumes so but doesn't know for sure.

"I'll hang out with her. We'll stay for an hour and then ditch them for some takeout on our way home. But be forewarned, if that bitch Jessica comes after me again, I can't be held responsible if the contents of my drinking glass become a weapon."

Rowen scowls at me. "This is why I don't want to go. She better not lay a finger on you, or we'll have some serious problems."

I wave him off. "I'm not worried about it. If we time it right, she'll be falling down drunk by the time we even get there."

He hrmphs and sits back in his seat. I stretch again. My back is really hurting now, and I wish the doctor would show up.

Speak of the devil, a quite rap on the door and it swings open, Dr. Hermann making his way in. "Tiffany, good to see you." Turning to Rowen he adds, "I'm Dr. Hermann."

"Rowen. Nice to meet you."

The good doc takes two quick steps to the sink where he does a quick wash of his hands. "I hear congratulations are in order."

His smile is so genuine, he puts me more at ease, although not totally.

"I'm not sure congratulations is the right word," I say sheepishly.

Sitting down on the chair, he grabs my chart and rolls forward. "It's not uncommon to feel like that. Babies have a way of surprising us and showing up when we least expect them."

"You got that right," I grumble, Rowen unaffected by my bad mood.

"Ignore her," my husband adds. "The sound of the paper on the table made her cranky."

I shoot him a glare, but Dr. Hermann doesn't seem to notice. "Well, that's an easy enough fix. We'll just lay a sheet down on it next time you're here," he says as he jots something down in the paperwork. "I see you have a new last name now too. Wow. There are a lot of congratulations in this room today. Did this happen before or after the new addition?"

"A couple months before," Rowen answers quickly. Not that it matters to me, but I'm sure he wants to make it very clear that this was done in the traditional order. I just shake my head in amusement.

"Oh, well then I can see why this is such a big surprise. Lie down for me, Tiffany." Dr. Hermann continues to ask basic questions about things like my morning sickness that has hit with a vengeance while he presses on my abdomen and does a quick breast exam. Rowen shifts in his seat, obviously uncomfortable with another man touching my breasts, but he's going to have to get over it. Dr. Hermann is about to see a whole lot of more of me over the next few months.

"Everything feels good." I chance a glance at Rowen and try not to laugh that he clearly doesn't appreciate the doctor's choice of words after having his hands on my boobs. Dr. Hermann doesn't notice as he pulls the stirrups out from under the table. "Let's go ahead and get your feet in these so we can get a better idea of your due date. Rowen, can you hit the lights for me?"

The room goes dark as the monitor comes on.

"This is going to feel just like a pelvic exam," Dr. Hermann warns as he holds up a thin wand with a condom over it. "Except there won't be a pinch at the end. Just hold still and let's take a look."

I suck in a breath as he inserts the wand inside of me. Rowen is immediately by my side and grabs my hand, staring intently at the screen. In just seconds, cloudy shapes begin flashing across the screen as Dr. Hermann moves the wand around. Then he stops. And just one picture lights up the screen.

"And there is your baby."

Rowen's hand tightens around mine, but I barely notice. I'm too focused on the fluttering happening inside the jelly bean. It's such a strange picture, yet I have the oddest thought that it's the most beautiful thing I've ever seen.

We watch as Dr. Hermann takes some measurements and notates the heart rate. All the while, I'm mesmerized by what I'm seeing. That tiny thing is going to be my baby. *Our* baby. I'm fascinated and excited and afraid. But mostly I'm just in awe.

"You are measuring eight weeks, three days pregnant."

"Wow. That far along?" I ask. How could I have been pregnant for two months and never even realized it?

"That's what the baby says." He smiles up at me, immediately turning his attention back to the screen. "I'm estimating your due date is around August sixteenth."

Suddenly, the screen goes blank as Dr. Hermann pulls the wand away and snaps his gloves off. Looking over at Rowen for the first time since the exam began, he looks stunned. Like he can't believe it's real. When I kiss his hand clasped in mine, his gaze catches mine—and he smiles. A bright, excited, overjoyed smile.

I know in that moment, this may not be great timing, but it's exactly the way our lives were supposed to go.

"Everything looks good," Dr. Hermann announces, standing up and washing his hands again. "The nurse is going to come in with some samples of prenatal vitamins. I want to see you in another month to check on how you're doing, and we'll continue on from there. Sound good?" He tosses a now wet paper towel into the trash. We nod in response, both of us still too stunned to talk. By the knowing smile that crosses his face, it appears we're not the first couple to be stunned silent.

He claps Rowen on the back and flips on the light, giving us another congratulations and handing Rowen some copies of the ultrasound pictures I didn't realize he printed on his way out the door.

Rowen stares at the pictures for a solid minute before looking at me, tears filling his eyes.

"I love you, *mo chuisle*," Rowen breathes, his forehead gently dropping to mine.

It's a new term of endearment I haven't heard before. But in this moment, it's officially my favorite.

CHAPTER 8

Rowen

"I can't believe we're doing this," I grumble, the sounds of what is obviously an over-the-top party already making me itchy, and we're not even to the front door yet. Makes me wonder what all the neighbors are thinking and when they'll be calling the cops.

Nate Funderling and his giant ego bought an overpriced condo a couple of years ago, right near Memorial Drive. Knowing what professional soccer players make, I know it was way over his budget, and I've always wondered how he was able to buy it in the first place.

Now that he's moving to Timbuktu, instead of selling it, he's renting it out. My guess is he'll be upside down on the mortgage if he doesn't hold on to it for a while longer. Because he's a dumb ass. So instead of being able to unload it, he's renting it to… hell I don't know who he's renting it to, nor do I care. I stopped interacting with most of my teammates beyond necessary team conversation after several of them participated in publicly humiliating Tiffany.

Posting a naked picture on social that she didn't even know was taken, and then plastering copies all over the locker room, wasn't just unnecessary, it effectively ruined any respect I had for several members of my team. Sure, I'll hang out with Daniel and Christian and the happily married crowd of guys almost twice my age. But everyone else can go fuck themselves, as far as I'm concerned.

I may have gotten my even-keeled nature from my mom. But my ability to hold a grudge came from my pure-blood Irish father. Just like him, you can mess with me and I'll probably forgive you. Mess with the love of my life? That is one bridge that hasn't just been burned. Oh no. It's been torched, vaporized, and the land it was built on is as toxic as Chernobyl. There is no fixing it. Ever.

That's probably why I have such a hard time with Santos still. He never went as far as the others, but he went far enough.

All that being said, I have no idea who the fuck will live here once the Fuckerlings are gone. I don't even know who the fuck is here now.

"It'll be fine." Tiffany grabs my hand and pulls me to her, her arms wrapping around my neck while I pout. "We'll make the rounds so we're seen. Extend our best wishes to the Fund—"

"Nope," I cut her off. "We're not giving those assholes our best."

She rolls her eyes but continues. "Fine. We'll avoid Nate and Jessica and just talk to a few people. Have one drink. Thirty minutes, in and out for appearances."

I sigh heavily and draw her tighter to me. The feeling of her calms me, but not by much. I'm wound too tight. "Fine. But since you're making me do this, I get to choose our position tonight." A deep laugh rumbles through her when I squeeze her ass. "There's this thing I wanna try involving a reverse cowgirl."

"Hmm," she says seductively. "Someone is turning into an ass man."

"I've always been an ass man around you," I say, smacking her on said appendage, which makes her shriek, then pulling away to walk hand in hand to the door.

Rapping on it once, Tiffany pushes it open without waiting for someone to answer. It's like my nightmare come true— bringing my wife back into this scene.

There are people everywhere. Not just players, but the groupie crowd is in full effect as well. Scantily clad women are doing body shots off each other and some heavy make-out sessions have already commenced. I was hoping Jessica's WAG friends would be here to deter some of the crazy, but it looks like they either left early or didn't bother to come at all.

Grabbing Tiffany's shoulder and squeezing, she looks up at me and smiles with resignation, her earlier bravado fading. She doesn't want to be here anymore than I do.

"Thirty minutes," I grumble in her ear. "Time starts now."

"It's the Flanigan's!" We look up as Daniel comes barreling toward us, hugging Tiffany and then pulling me into a headlock, unlit stogie hanging out of his mouth.

"Is Quincy here?" Tiffany asks, and Daniel finally releases me, turning his attention toward her.

"Nah. Babysitter cancelled at the last minute."

Tiffany quirks an eyebrow at him. "Uh huh. Funny how that happens every time one of these parties come up."

He smiles and lifts his eyebrows back. "What can I say? The kid comes first."

Tiffany just shakes her head, trying to hide her amusement. We all know it's an excuse to not have to darken the doors of a Mutiny party. This really isn't any of our scenes. So we chat for a few minutes about Quincy's move and how many times Daniel has woken up with a baby foot in his face in the last week. The stories are more entertaining than they used to be, probably because it makes me wonder what my own life will be like in a year. I bite my lip, holding back a goofy grin. That would be a dead giveaway that something's up, and I'm not ready to share this just yet.

Looking down at her, I notice Tiffany's starting to look kind of squeamish.

"You okay?" I whisper in her ear when Daniel gets distracted by a ruckus coming from the other room. I don't know what's happening in there, but based on previous experience, I'm not interested in finding out.

She looks up at me and nods, but it's clear she doesn't mean it. "Can you see if there's any Sprite or ginger ale. Something bubbly like that?"

"Nauseous?" She closes her eyes and nods once, leaning into me. "Do we need to leave?"

She shakes her head. "No. But I'm gonna go find a place to sit down."

I kiss her on the top of the head and watch her push through the crowd away from me. I know she's fine and being here isn't that big of a deal. But I'm not too proud to admit I'm still uncomfortable with her in this situation again. Hell, with both of us in this situation again. And now even more so that my child is with us.

My child. So much for keeping that goofy grin hidden.

Heading into the kitchen, I run into the new rookie, Logan Morose. Bumped up from the farm team, he joined us just last week. That's not a lot of time to mesh with everyone and from his body language, I'm not sure he wants to.

"What's up, man?" I nod my head at him as I open the fridge and begin looking around.

"Not much."

"You enjoying the party?"

When he doesn't answer, I look up to see him running his fingers through his hair nervously. "Are all the parties like this?"

Grabbing a Shiner and a Sprite, I put the soda on the counter, so I can twist the beer top open and toss the top in the trash. "You mean loud, obnoxious, and full of drunk people?"

"Yeah."

I take a swig and shake my head. "Nope. Usually they're worse."

"Really?" He grimaces. Interesting that he's uncomfortable. And a little confusing as well. Most times the new guy is more than excited to party with the team, but not Logan.

I don't know him well yet, but so far, he hasn't come across as a self-righteous douche. Not in practice. Not in the locker room. And now, not here. Maybe I need to give him the benefit of the doubt.

"I take it this isn't really your scene?"

He shakes his head. "Not at all. I guess I should have expected it, but in the semi-pros we were all so focused on trying to get to this level, we didn't really do… this," he says with a wave of his hand.

"Or maybe because you were in BFE and wasn't anywhere to do it without getting caught?"

He smiles at my assessment and tips his beer at me. "That could be it too. Or that we were in a dry county."

I throw my hand over my mouth as I choke on my drink. "They still have those?" I cough out.

He grins. "You'd be surprised what kind of interesting things still go on in the deep South."

"Houston isn't deep South?"

"Not south enough," he jokes and then sighs. "I guess I'll get used to the culture shock eventually."

"Nah." I lean against the counter and cross my ankles, settling in for a few. It's much more comfortable in here where there isn't as much noise and you can actually hold a conversation. "No one's gonna judge you if you never come to another one of these things. It's not my scene either. More like a show of camaraderie. I've already set my timer. Just"—I glance down at my watch and back up—"twenty-five more minutes until I can convince the wife to leave."

"I haven't met your wife yet. Tiffany, right?" he asks and takes a swig of his own beer.

"Yep. She's around here somewhere." A loud ruckus coming from the living room reminds me that it's probably not a good idea to leave her alone for much longer. As much as I trust her, these dicks are still drinking like fish, and I'd rather be next to her, just in case, than have regrets later. "Anyway"—I push off the counter and grab the Sprite—"I have a drink to deliver. But listen, a few of us who do not enjoy all this"—I gesture out to the party sounds again—"have a regular poker night. Just booze, cigars, and a bunch of trash talk. If you're interested, I'll let ya know next time we have one."

The way his face relaxes, I can tell a guy's night around a poker table is much more his style.

"Yeah. Yeah that'd be great, thanks."

"Cool."

We head out of the kitchen and part ways, Logan turning toward a quiet corner and me making my way through the crowd. Searching the living room and dining room, I still can't find Tiffany. Could she have gone to lie down in one of the bedrooms?

Pushing through a door in the back, I enter what looks like a guest room and see a sliding glass door ahead of me. Through the glass, I see my wife sitting across from Santos. Immediately, my hackles rise. I put the can of Sprite down as I head toward the door. If he's starting shit with her again, I want my hands free, so I can make good on my last threat.

Sliding the door open, they both look up at me.

"Everything okay out here, babe?"

"Fine," Tiffany assures and reaches for me. Seeing the question in my eyes, she continues with, "Sorry. The smoke was getting to me."

I nod once and gesture for her to move forward so I can sit behind her. Partially to be near her and partially to remind Santos that her place is with me. He's not looking at us, but I'm not dumb enough to think he doesn't see it.

"Babe, can I ask you a question?" Tiffany asks. I nod as I shift and get more comfortable. "How did you know I was done with this lifestyle? With the parties and stuff."

The personal nature of her question surprises me. I'm not really sure how to answer, especially in front of present company.

"Um, I.. I don't know," I stutter.

She nudges me. "Come on. I promise I'm not being girly and emotional right now. I need your honest answer."

I'm still not convinced but I don't mind humoring her. Leaning my head back, I think about how best to answer. "Well, I guess it's because we'd talked about being monogamous."

"And you just trusted me?"

I cringe. This is one of those questions where I'm damned if I do and damned if I don't. I might as well go for it. I suspect she's trying to make a point about something so it's best to run with it. Even if it backfires and I don't get that reverse cowgirl later. "Well, not at first. But I guess the longer we were together and the more you proved good on your word, the more I trusted you."

She turns to look at me. "Did you hear that, Santos?"

"I'm not sure what that has to do with me," Santos grumbles.

What the hell kind of conversation did I walk in on?

"You and Mariana just got divorced. But that doesn't mean your relationship is over. If you want to be a different guy, be it."

He snorts humorlessly. "Thanks for the vote of confidence, but she doesn't want anything to do with me."

"That's where you're wrong." Tiffany turns her entire body to face him. I don't like losing the heat of her against me, but she's on a roll right now. "She doesn't want anything to do with the guy who cheated on her without a second thought. She doesn't want anything to do with the pain that makes her feel. But if you are a different person, truly have that part of your life under control, there's no reason you can't get back together."

I stare at her for a few seconds thinking about how amazing it is that not only does she not blame Santos for the shitty way he talks to her sometimes but is sitting here actually trying to help him. And then he ruins it by bursting out laughing.

"Are you kidding me right now?" he asks angrily, obviously missing her point. "Tiffany, we went to a huge conference where we did the most intense therapy you can do. And that wasn't enough. I promised complete and total transparency and to never, ever fall off the wagon again. That wasn't enough. It's over and done with. She made that clear."

"I don't believe that," she argues firmly.

"How? How can you not believe that? She said no. She went to court and finalized the divorce."

"Because my cousin remarried her cheating husband."

Santos freezes with his glass halfway to his mouth. Pretty sure I have the same stunned expression on my face. For as well as I know my wife, I guess I missed a few details.

"Really?" A twinge of hope crosses Santos's face.

She nods. "Really. They were divorced for two years before he finally pulled his head out of his ass. He went through another year of therapy, proved he was a different man, a better man, and they got back together. They've been happily remarried for five years."

We watch as Santos digests the information. I can almost see the lightbulb that has finally come on. The one that shows him he *does* have choices. He *can* change his path. There's no telling if it'll make a different in his now defunct marriage, but isn't the point to better yourself before you can be your best for someone else?

"I see your point," Santos finally says, making Tiffany smile.

"Good." She pats me on the thigh. "Now if you'll excuse us, this baby mama is getting really, really tired all the sudden."

My eyes widen. We agreed not to tell anyone about the baby yet somehow Santos knows? "Babe!"

"He guessed."

Santos chuckles. "Don't worry. I'm not telling anyone. I've done this before, remember? That first trimester… phew… it's exciting and terrifying all at once."

"And exhausting and annoying," Tiffany tacks on. She stands up and I humor her by letting her think pulling on my hands is helping me to my feet as well.

"Hey, Rookie," Santos calls, using the nickname I haven't answered to in over a year. I stop and looks at him, unsure where this conversation is about to go. "Congratulations, man. I'm happy for you." He bumps fists with me and I feel a certain relief. Relief that someone else knows the best secret I've ever kept and is excited for me. And relief that maybe Santos is finally seeing the error of his ways and he's going to stop being a dick. Maybe he *can* earn my respect back. With that thought, I extend an olive branch I know he'll appreciate.

"Thanks, man. I just hope I'm as good of a dad as you are."

Placing my hand on Tiffany's lower back, we head back into the party.

"He and I still aren't going to be friends, ya know?"

"I know," Tiffany replies as we push our way through the crowd. "But we can still be kind to him when he's hurting."

Grabbing her, I pull her to me and kiss her deeply, not caring whose around. "You know how much I love you, right?"

She nods. "I do. Now get me out of her. I need to throw up before we get it on."

My chin drops to my chest as she turns tail and races out to the bushes.

CHAPTER

9

Tiffany

Pregnancy is not all it's cracked up to be. Not that I was expecting it to be a cakewalk. But I'd looked up a few websites and every one of them said morning sickness usually tapers off at about ten weeks or so.

Lies. They all tell lies.

Here I sit at twelve weeks pregnant, and not only has the nausea not gone away, I swear I throw up more now than I did a few weeks ago. Even these gross hard ginger candies my mother-in-law told me about don't work.

Disgusted at the thought of eating another one, I toss the offending candy back in my drawer and slam it shut just as Steve jumps out of his chair, arms raised victoriously.

"Woo hoo! Nailed it! Did you see that three-pointer?" he yells, eyes still glued to the monitor. "Nailed it!"

"Yep," I answer nonchalantly, even though I want to call him out about this catchphrase he's been overusing lately, but I don't. He knows basketball is my least favorite sport of them all. Especially these days when watching players run up and down on the court, back and forth on the screen, over and over and *over*, makes me want to toss my cookies.

He drops his arms in defeat. "You don't sound very excited. That was an impressive shot. He had two defenders on him."

"You know basketball isn't my jam."

Steve roars with laughter. "You said jam. About basketball. Your puns crack me up."

I smirk. I wasn't trying to be funny, I don't even get the joke, but if it keeps him entertained, I'm not going to pretend it was a mistake. As long as he's distracted and happy, I don't have to tell him what's really going on.

For a while now, I have been avoiding sharing the news of what's happening inside my body. Not because I don't trust Steve. I do. He's a phenomenal boss. But I'm still trying to keep this pregnancy under wraps until I'm out of the "danger zone."

At least, that's what I keep telling myself. While that's part of the reason, the other part is selfish. I want to find out what happens with Steve's job first. If he gets that position in New York, then his job will come open and I want it. Badly. Sports producer in a market this size by the ripe old age of twenty-four would be a giant step closer to my long-term dream of working for ESPN. But I'm not stupid. As much as the corporate world is starting to break open that glass ceiling, we all know it's damn near impossible to get a job when you're pregnant. No one wants to fill a position, only to have to refill it temporarily for maternity leave. It sucks, but I work in a male-dominated industry. I know how it works.

Getting back to my search of yesterday's late-night game scores, I feel the tell-tale signs of nausea rolling in again.

"Um, I'll be right back." I race out of the room, thankful that Steve doesn't look up. He never asks where I'm headed when I leave suddenly, and I'm grateful he never seems to pay attention enough to his surroundings to realize my bathrooms breaks have tripled recently.

This is also one of the times I'm glad the sports department is stuck upstairs. It's us and three reporters whose desks don't fit in the newsroom. That means the ladies restroom never has anyone in it except me.

After giving myself a few minutes to unload the oh-so-filling lunch I ate of crackers, I head back to my workstation. I guess I'll be sucking on another one of those disgusting candies after all.

Steve still doesn't seem to notice me coming back in, too busy writing up the story about the game he was just watching. So his next comment shocks the shit out of me.

"Are you ever going to tell me you're pregnant, or are you just waiting for me to figure it out on my own?"

Swiveling around in my chair, I cock my head at him. "I'm sorry—what?"

Looking me dead in the eye, he continues. "You heard me."

I open my mouth to respond, then close it. Denial won't work. I guess he pays more attention to his surroundings than I thought.

"I was hoping you wouldn't figure it out."

He continues doing the hunt and peck on his keyboard, not at all offended by my lack of disclosure. "This ain't my first rodeo with morning sickness, kid."

I purse my lips, but he waves me off. If anyone else called me "kid" I might be offended, but Steve is just inappropriate like that.

"Meg upchucked all the time when she was pregnant. Morning, afternoon, night, middle of sex." I grimace, but he doesn't notice. "She was miserable."

"You realize you just told me having sex with you made her throw up."

He pauses momentarily then shrugs. "I'm sure she's not the first to say that about me. Anyway"—I facepalm myself—"my point is you need to throw that nasty ass candy away and get a lemon."

Furrowing my brow, I'm trying to figure out what he's even talking about. "A lemon? Is this some weird reference to making lemonade or something stupid like that?"

"While that would have been a good one, no. This is about how sniffing a lemon cancels out all the other smells around you and calms the tummy. In fact…" He reaches into his drawer and rummages around for a few seconds. "Ah ha! Here it is. I brought you this."

Handing me a lemon triumphantly, I can't help but be touched by his gesture. Not only is he not upset I didn't tell him about the pregnancy, he brought me something to feel better anyway. I might have a stray tear or two if I wasn't too busy sniffing my new anti-nausea medication.

"I hope this works. Thank you so much."

"Wait. Give it back." He reaches his hands and wiggles his fingers like it's of the utmost importance that he takes back his gift. So I comply. I have no idea what he has up his sleeve now.

Putting the lemon on his desk, he grabs his lunch fork and stabs the shit out of the fruit making me jump. "Here." He hands it back to me. "You get more of the scent that way."

Sure enough, as I hold it up to my nose and breath normally, my nausea fades away.

"Ohmygod, that's so much better."

"Nailed it."

"What is it with you and that catchphrase?"

He shrugs. "It fits so many parts of my life." I roll my eyes as he continues spouting off all his positive traits. "Including the fact that I'm a wealth of pregnancy information," he boasts, going back to his work. "You should've been picking my brain all along."

"It seems that way."

"And don't worry. When the horrific gas that smells like something is rotting inside you comes, I have remedies for that too."

Shaking my head, I try not to laugh. "I'm gonna pretend you didn't just say that."

"Pretend all you want. Eventually you'll let one rip during a staff meeting and be pissed at yourself for not taking me up on my offer."

"Okay, I'm gonna just keep gathering these scores…"

He shrugs as I turn back to my monitor, keeping the lemon close by. Admittedly, I feel a little stupid. Part of my job is researching. Researching scores, background information on players, patterns of play for teams. And yet I couldn't figure out how to look up remedies for morning sickness? I'm losing my touch.

Steve spends the next hour watching the game from last night I have no interest in. I already know who won thanks to the highlight reel I scoured hours ago. It took two minutes to find what we need for tonight instead of two hours. But while basketball may be my least favorite sport, it's his most favorite. To each his own, I suppose.

Suddenly, Steve gets quiet. A little too quiet. He's not silent. I still hear him moving around. But his normal outbursts and clicking of the keys aren't there.

"Tiffany," he practically growls, immediately putting me on edge.

Spinning around a little too quickly, I take a quick sniff of my lemon. When my stomach calms down, I look up at him. He's just staring at me, mouth open, eyes wide.

"You're scaring me. What's wrong?"

He shakes his head, like he can't believe what he's about to say. "They want to interview me."

Just like that, my own jaw drops open. "You mean—?"

He nods. "New York wants to interview me."

My hands fly up to cover my mouth. Now my eyes are wide as well. "Are you kidding me?"

"Nope." He stands slowly, annunciating each word as he goes up. "I. Have. An. Interview. In. NEW YORK!"

He throws his head back and bellows his excitement, and I join him with my own cheers of excitement. Good thing we get loud up here regularly. I'm sure no one downstairs is even flinching at our outburst.

"When? When do they want to see you?" I ask excitedly.

He leans over to read off what I presume is an email. "Uh, looks like next week. Think you can come in on Sunday night, just in case my plane runs late?"

"Hell, yeah," I say without hesitation. "This is too important. Ohmygod, Steve, you're being interviewed in the number one market in the country!"

He flops down on his chair and looks up at the ceiling. "I can't believe it. I thought there wasn't a shot in hell."

"Of course there was." He bats away the wadded-up piece of paper I throw at him. "You're an amazing producer in a market that has almost every professional sport right here in town. I bet they were thrilled to get your résumé."

He blows out a breath, still shaking his head in disbelief. "You know if I get it, you need to put in for this job, right?"

I shouldn't be surprised by his words, but I am. It's one thing to be told you're good at your job. It's another thing for your boss to come out and say he wants you to be his successor.

Feeling a little weepy after all the excitement, I barely croak out, "Yes."

"Good." He sits up straight and raps his knuckles on his desk. "Because I don't want this department going to shit. We need strong leadership and someone who knows what the hell they're doing. That's you."

"While I appreciate your vote of confidence, you know you aren't the deciding factor, right? Even if you do get the job in New York, and I have this feeling you will, there are no guarantees the bigwigs will want to move me up."

"Don't sell yourself short. They know what you can do."

"Yeah, but they don't know I'm pregnant yet," I admit. "You know that might put a kink in it."

Gotta love, Steve. His face immediately looks like I've said the dumbest thing ever. "You're kidding, right?"

"Oh, come on. You know full well HR won't want to mess with maternity leave paperwork."

He gives me the once-over with his eyes, which is weird, but knowing Steve he probably thinks there is a point to it. "Seems to me you're going to be filling out that paperwork one way or the other."

"Is that why you just looked me up and down like a creeper?"

"I was trying to prove that you're going to look pregnant either way. Get it now?"

"No."

"Hmm. I missed the mark on that one."

I drop my head in my hands. I can only hope whoever he interviews with finds his weird sense of humor as endearing as I do.

"My point is, glass ceiling or not, you already work here. It's not like you would start and three months later take time off. It's not a big deal."

My eyebrows shoot up. "It is a big deal, Steve."

"Well, yeah. It's a baby and all that crap. But it's not a big deal like you think. Remember last year when that picture came out?"

I bristle. The last thing I expected was for Steve to ever talk about that horrible time again. I know my face is flaming, and I've gone stiff.

"Stop looking like that," he interjects. "I've still never looked at it, so whatever. I don't care what you do on your off time, although please never speak to me of your sexual escapades."

"Hold up. Didn't you just tell me your wife used to throw up after having sex with you?"

He rolls his eyes in exasperation. "Tiffany, you are losing focus on the issue."

Now it's my turn to roll my eyes.

"Management could have thrown you under the bus because of some random morality clause none of us knew about or something. But they didn't. They recognize your value and why you are important to this organization. If I get this job, no. *When* I get this job, I'm putting in my recommendation for you to take over here." He turns back to his screen, pointing at me one last time. "Get ready, kid. Big things are happening for both of us."

He goes back to his work and leaves me to my own thoughts.

I want this job. I want it so badly I can taste it. But how is this all going to work with a baby coming? I can't take time off every time Rowen goes out of town. Is there even a twenty-four-hour daycare? And do I want my child to go there?

Steve is right. Big things are happening. I just don't know if they're going to end up overwhelming me.

CHAPTER
10

It's funny how everything changes when you find the one you want to be with forever.

Two years ago, going on a road trip was fun. I liked visiting different cities and checking out stadiums around the country. I enjoyed hanging out with my teammates. We had a good time.

Then Tiffany and I started dating and it got harder. I still enjoyed going on trips, but I always wanted to get back quickly to be with her. I wasn't clingy or anything. Nothing stalkerish. With her is just where I wanted to be all the time.

Now that she's pregnant, though, I have no desire to leave whatsoever. None. My instincts have kicked in something fierce, and all I want to do is stay home and take care of her. It doesn't help that she's sick all the time. It just increases my worry tenfold. Even when she tries to make me feel better.

"Seriously, Rookie, I'm fine."

"You aren't fine, babe. I can tell by your voice that you just got sick again."

Sitting on the bench in the locker room, I'm taking advantage of the fact that everyone else is either showering, milling about, or wasting time on the field and not here yet. No one is listening to this conversation.

"You can't tell that by my voice."

"Yes, I can. You sound raspier."

"Well that's—gross. Besides, I get sick all the time, Rowen. That doesn't mean I'm not fine."

Sighing, I rub my hand down my face. "I know that. But I hate seeing you like this. I wish I could do more to make it better."

She laughs lightly. "You worry too much. You heard the doctor. This is normal. It just might take a couple more weeks before the sickness goes away."

"Are you sure you want me to go on this road trip, though? I'm gonna be gone for close to a week. I could always take a leave of absence—"

"Shut up, Rookie," she demands. I immediately stop talking. I'm no dummy. Tiffany doesn't snap at me often, but when she does, she's serious. "We're not going to rearrange our entire lives because of a pregnancy. That comes after the baby gets here. Quit your bitching and do your job. You have games to win."

I can't help but chuckle at her demanding tone. "Yes, ma'am."

"And don't patronize me."

Now she has me smiling. "Okay, okay. I'll back off. No guarantees I won't ask again tomorrow, though."

"Fine," she concedes. "But just be prepared for me to be pissy then too."

"Understood."

I hear shouting in the background through the phone, probably Steve, which is my cue to let her go.

"Sounds like you're getting busy."

"I wouldn't call it busy." She audibly sighs. "Steve is a little too excited about basketball season. Thank God your season just started too. I was almost ready to quit my job just so I didn't have to hear anything else about this year's upcoming Slam Dunk contest."

I chuckle, watching as Santos finally comes in. When I walked off the field, he was getting his ass handed to him by coach. No idea what kind of mood he's in. He doesn't seem agitated. Maybe they worked out a training plan, or something.

"I hear ya. Well, get back to work, babe. I love you. Throw up and all."

"Love you too."

We hang up, just as my teammate reaches his own locker next to mine.

"You ready to hit the road in a couple days, Rowen?" Santos takes a seat on the bench next to me and begins the tedious process of unwrapping all the athletic tape off his body. I make a mental note as I unwrap my own ankles to never take my age for granted. Someday, I'll be taping up every part of myself as well.

"I don't normally mind these long stretches. But Tiffany hasn't been feeling well," I explain quietly, not wanting anyone to overhear. "I don't like leaving her behind."

Santos stops unwrapping and looks around, making sure no one else is listening. I appreciate that he's making sure this information is going to stay between us. "Everything okay with the baby?" Taking my cue, he speaks as quietly as I am.

I nod, but I'm sure the expression on my face matches it. "So far. We had a doctor's appointment yesterday and she's officially twelve weeks." That part makes me smile a little. Just remembering what our little baby looks like on that screen makes me all kinds of happy. If no one else was around, I'd pull up the picture I took on my phone and show him. Hell, I'm seriously considering doing it anyway, just because I want to look at again myself.

Santos's smile indicates he completely understands my excitement. But I guess he would. He's got three kids of his own. Even after all the shit that led to his divorce, there was never a question in anyone's mind that he's a fantastic father. "That's great, man. You're almost done with the first tri-mester."

"I know, that's why I'm worried." I use a little too much force to toss my own tape into the trash and rest my hands on my knees, ready to tell all. "All that morning sickness is sup-posed to go away by ten or twelve weeks, but it seems to be getting worse. We asked about it yesterday and the doctor said some women never get over it."

"Seriously?"

"It doesn't happen often, but of course it happens to my wife. And, *of course,* there's nothing I can do about it. And, *of course,* the doctor mentioned watching for dehydration since she throws up a thousand times a day, so now I feel like I'm constantly making her drink water, which just makes her throw up again." The frustration runs through me again, now that I'm not having to hold myself together in front of Tiffany. Not that I need to, but I know it adds to her aggravation these days.

"I'm sorry, man. That fucking sucks."

"I don't know how you went through this three times," I

say with a shake of my head.

He chuckles. "It's different every time. I remember the first time, Mari felt great. She would exercise every day and had lots of energy. With Lina, it was the exact opposite. She was tired and felt horrible."

That piques my interest. "Lots of morning sickness?"

"None, actually. She said she just felt gross for nine straight months. Like when you just have a small fever, not enough to knock you on your ass, but enough for it to make everyday activities miserable. She said that's what it felt like."

"What about the last time?"

He laughs, like he's enjoying this quick walk down memory lane. "She was huge. I mean, you saw her that one time at Daniel's party."

I grin. "She was pretty big."

"She still had a couple months to go then. And the closer she got, ohmygod, she turned into a raging lunatic."

Furrowing my brow, I look at him. "Wait… Mari? Your wife, uh… ex-wife Mari was a lunatic?"

Fortunately, he ignores my faux pas and continues on like I didn't just verbally punch him in the gut. "Yep. My Mari. The sweetest, kindest, most wonderful woman I've ever known in my life cussed like a sailor and had terrible road rage."

I can't help but bark out of laugh. The thought of Mariana being anything but friendly seems almost ridiculous. "I don't believe you."

"Believe it." He smiles as he continues telling me all about when his kids were born. "The girls were the only people she was nice to. Everyone else could suck it. She made the grocery store cashier cry at one point for putting dishwasher detergent in the same bag as the bread. It was insane. And then one day, a couple months after Theo was born, it was like the switch was flipped, and she was back to my sweet wife."

He smiles at the memory. It's nice seeing him happy. Well, maybe not happy, but at least content. Maybe Tiffany was right when she said he just needed some time to get over the hurt and anger. Maybe I was too quick to judge him. I know he apologized to Tiffany for his outburst, which I appreciated. But maybe this particular bridge can be rebuilt. We were all hurt when Santos's marriage fell apart. It affected a lot of us in various ways.

"That pregnancy was really rough," he continues. "But it was totally worth it."

"Is it weird that I can already hardly wait for him to be born?"

His eyebrows shoot up. "Him? You already know?"

I nod, and I'm sure a blush is creeping up my face. It always does whenever I feel a strong emotion, and really, nothing has ever felt as strong as my excitement over my son. "She had a blood test a couple of weeks ago for some other things and they could tell that way."

"You're having a son?" His smile widens as I nod again. "Congratulations, man." He slaps me on the back and I swear my face is on fire now. "That's great news."

"What's great news?" Daniel asks, throwing his cleats in his locker with a bang.

Nope. Not gonna go there right now. Santos is one thing. He gets it. But the rest of them can wait for a while.

"Oh, uh, my parents have decided to find a place down here," I retort quickly, stripping off the rest of my clothes and wrapping a towel around my waist. "I can't wait for her to cook for me on a regular basis. I love Tiffany, but good god, that woman can't cook for shit."

Daniel shakes his head, eyes glazed over as he thinks. "Yeah, there's nothing like your mama's home cooking. Have I ever told you about my mama's enchiladas?"

Christian groans as he strips. "I'm already hungry. Don't talk about my favorite meal. It's gonna make that protein shake I have waiting for me taste like dirt."

Daniel makes a face. "It tastes like dirt because you put too many greens in it. Why don't you just blend a bunch of dried up leaves instead."

Christian throws a sock in Daniel's face making him squeal like a little girl, and it's on. I know better than to stick around for the wrestling match. Instead, I head for the showers to think.

The biggest question on my mind is how I can take care of my wife while I'm gone. Surely there's something I can do to make her life easier. My parents will be flying in tomorrow, so maybe I can elicit my mam's help. If she can make some plain rice and noodles to put in the fridge for Tiffany to eat while I'm gone, that means she won't have to cook. It's a far cry from bangers and mash, but it's better than nothing.

I make another mental note, this one to stop by the store and grab some crackers, ginger ale, and lemons on my way home. And I can wash the sheets tomorrow before packing, to make sure she's got fresh bedding.

This pregnancy is not what we expected, and it's already starting out harder than we'd hoped. But this is what partners do—they help ease the burden for each other. And if a little bit of bland food and clean sheets can make my wife more comfortable, I'm game.

This is the best thing that's ever happened to me. I never want Tiffany to feel like it's the worst.

CHAPTER 11

Tiffany

I underestimated the vastness of the housing market in Houston. By a lot.

Who knew when you have a decent-sized budget and a good realtor, you could spend hours upon hours searching for the perfect home?

I didn't. And now I regret it.

When Rowen's mom, Denise, invited me to come along with them, I reluctantly said yes. I am almost out of my first trimester, but the exhaustion and sickness is still taking a huge toll on me. I really wanted to nap instead, but they're my husband's parents. My child's grandparents. I want us to be close since they're going to be around so much more in the next few months.

Plus, a small part of me still feels like I'm trying to impress them. It's overcompensation for the embarrassment I still feel about our first meeting. I know I shouldn't feel that way. They've made it very clear they don't look at me differently or anything. But damn if that insecurity doesn't rear its ugly head if I think too hard. Hormones don't help.

So I agreed to go house hunting, assuming it meant seeing a couple places and then calling it a day for lunch.

Oh, how wrong I was. We ended up touring at least a dozen different places all over town. It took hours to get from one side of Houston to the other to see them all. And I'm still not sure we did it because the realtor scheduled them all for today to be efficient, or if it's because Ryan demanded they find something immediately. He can be kind of obnoxious that way.

As evidenced by the fact that he and Denise are trying to narrow down their options, but still can't agree because of one little thing.

"I think the condo is perfect." Ryan's thick Irish accent bleeds through. "It's gated and has that little courtyard thingy—"

"It was a two-by-two grass patch, Ryan," Denise interjects, as she pours some ginger into the rice she's making. I have no idea what she's cooking, but it smells good. "I would hardly call it a courtyard."

"No," Ryan concedes, arms crossed over his broad chest as he debates. "But it's a big enough area for me to stretch on the way to me run and a place to take off me sweaty clothes on the way back before hittin' the shower."

Denise turns the heat up on the rice and opens the fridge, talking loudly over her shoulder as she digs around on the shelves.

"They have a place just like that in the brownstone. I'm

sure you've heard of it. It's called a *laundry room*," she emphasizes, turning back with a carton of eggs in her hands. "And the best part is you can throw those sweaty clothes right in the washer instead of on the grass."

He harrumphs. "In the condo, I don't have to maintain a yard."

"In the brownstone, I don't have to vacuum stairs."

They come to a standstill, and I find myself giggling.

"What's so funny, *banchliamhain*?"

I slowly lift my head from where it was resting on my crossed arms. "I'm just trying to figure out how you're going to cut the grass in that tiny little courtyard. Are you gonna use scissors?"

Denise laughs lightly, placing the eggs in the bottom of a pot. Ryan, on the other hand, seems stumped.

"The lass has a point," he eventually says to Denise.

"She does," Denise agrees. "I think she also would feel more comfortable knowing her child is visiting a home that doesn't have stairs but does have a backyard he can play in."

Ryan grunts again and rubs the scruff on his face. "Ye really want that brownstone, aiy?"

She shrugs nonchalantly. "It's not about wanting the brownstone as much as it's about getting the right house for this season in our lives. Ryan, we aren't moving to Houston because it's been our retirement dream or anything. We're here to be with our family and to help raise our grandson. I want our home to be functional for that."

He sighs again before admitting defeat. "Alright, *Muirneach*. If that's the one ye think is best, let's put in an offer." He raises his finger as if he has an important point to make. "But I'm hiring a lawn guy. I won't be doin' the grass in this humidity."

Denise rolls her eyes at him but continues filling the pot with water. "Because pushing a lawn mower a couple times a month is so much harder than shoveling the snow every time we have a blizzard in Detroit??"

"I'm gettin' old, *grá mo chroí*. Need to save me energy for teachin' me *garmhac* how to kick the ball."

"Here we go again," Denise exclaims. "It's the same thing I heard for my entire pregnancy."

"What er ye goin' on about, woman?" Ryan jabs playfully, making her pop a towel at him.

"This child is goin' te be a football star, Denise," she mimics using her best impression of her husband's lilt. "Start training 'em young. Times a wastin'.'"

I chortle while Ryan feigns indifference.

"It worked, didn't it? Me boyo isn't here because he's on the road with his team, aiy?"

Denise gives him a glare over the bowl she has now pulled out. "I'll tell you the same thing I said twenty-five years ago. Show him how to play, but let him decide if it's his passion. This isn't even your child."

Ryan scoffs. "He's me garmhac. He might as well have come from me own loins."

I grimace and Denise smacks him on the arm. "Don't you have a game to watch or something? Something that means you'll be out of this room and out of my hair?"

He grumbles something I don't understand, probably in Gaelic, and kisses her on the head before leaving. But before he goes, he turns around quickly.

"Tiffany." I lift my eyes up to his and cock my head. "Why did the narcissist cross the road?"

Without delay I answer, "Because he thought it was a boundary."

"Dammit, I thought I had her," he mumbles under his breath as he turns to talk away.

Laying my head back on my arms, I notice Denise has a huge grin on her face.

"What?" I ask.

She glances up at me then back down to dump some flour in the bowl. "Every time he can't stump you makes me laugh. You know he actually jots down jokes now, so he can remember to try them out on you?" She chuckles. "It's become his personal mission to prove he's funnier than you."

I shake my head, stifling a giggle. "That is a very strange life goal."

"No one ever said my husband wasn't strange. He's a good man, but he definitely keeps me on my toes."

I watch as she reads her recipe and continues adding ingredients to the bowl. I'm not a very good cook, but I enjoy watching her do so many things at once. Rice, eggs, now… whatever this is. I'm impressed.

"Why don't you go take a nap," she says suddenly, and I realize I must look as wiped as I feel. My head is back down on my arms and I'm just blankly staring as she works.

"I should," I say through a deep sigh. "But I don't know if I have enough energy to climb off this stool. Did you feel like this when you had Rowen?"

She smirks at me. "No. I was one of those annoying women who felt fantastic the whole time I was pregnant. I loved it. The last two weeks were hard, but nothing like you're going through."

"Would it be wrong of me to say I hate you for that?"

Denise laughs lightly but doesn't look up. "You wouldn't be the first. I know how lucky I was. Plus, we were close to Ryan's family, so we had lots of support. I don't think I realized how good I had it. I recognize it now."

"I wanna be happy about being pregnant, but all the vomitting makes it hard."

"I know. And it's okay to not be happy right now. It doesn't mean you don't want this baby or you have regrets. It just means things are hard right now. But it'll get better."

Shifting so my chin is sitting on my arms, I ask the question that's been on my mind since I found out they were moving here. "What are your plans when you guys get here? As far as the baby goes." I wince. "That didn't come out right. I mean, I don't want to assume anything but I'm already trying to make plans and well, I'm not sure what you are hoping for."

"As far as babysitting goes?"

I nod, thankful she's so nonchalant.

"I have grandiose ideas in my mind about how much time I'll spend with my grandbaby."

I school my features because that sounds overwhelming. I must not do a very good job, though, because she laughs and pats my arm.

"But I know you have a life and family of your own, and we don't want to be any sort of imposition. Well, I can't guarantee Ryan won't show up on your doorstep unannounced one too many times, but Rowen can deal with him."

I groan because she's right. I could very easily imagine Ryan showing up every day to see his grandchild.

"Really, it's up to you, Tiffany. I'm ready to babysit five days a week if it'll help you out. But if you want to put the baby in daycare and just use us for date night, that's okay too."

Sitting up, I decide I need to level with her. And probably with myself too.

"I don't want to put him into daycare. It's fine and all, but for me—I don't know. It just isn't what I want." She nods in understanding. "But I'm not really, I guess I'm not used to family pitching in that much." Covering my face, I mumble, "That sounds really bad."

"Oh no, sweetie. I totally understand where you're coming from."

Peeking through my fingers, I say, "You do?"

"Oh yeah. I wasn't close to my parents growing up."

"Wait. I thought your whole family was in Detroit, and you guys were really tight."

"We are now. But that didn't happen until after we moved back to the States. I think being in Europe for as long as I was, my parents made more of an effort when we got back. Or maybe they were just older and wiser. I don't really know. But at your age, nope. We weren't *not* close. It just wasn't like Ryan's family."

She looks up and laughs, probably at a memory of the Flanigan clan.

"You think Ryan is a lot to handle? The rest of them were overwhelming when I first met them. No boundaries whatsoever. Everyone was in everyone's business all the time. And there were so many of them. It took some time to get used to having people to count on in a crisis. And not just a couple. It was like a whole tribe. I don't think I bought Rowen one single thing until he was three." She smiles at the memory. "So yes. I know exactly where you're coming from. But Tiffany, I'm not here to hover or be a helicopter grandma. I'm here to be *your* tribe. You have goals and dreams."

"I feel like I'm stuck in this weird place where I have to decide what is the most important—baby or career."

She shrugs. "If things were different, you might have to. But you don't. All you have to decide is if you want part-time daycare in the afternoon, or part-time grandma."

When she puts it that way, it really is that simple. I have my regular two days off, and Rowen has a day off when I work, which means it's only four days. Plus, with the way our schedules overlap, it's only until Rowen gets out of practice. Sometimes, that'll only be a couple of hours.

"You don't have to decide now. It's just something to keep in the back of your brain until he's born."

I nod as my thoughts continue to swirl. Not everyone is in a position where they can have it all, but I might be the exception to the rule. I continue to ponder all of this, when suddenly I catch the smell of a sweet aroma. I'm not sure what it is, but I'm guessing it's something on the stove.

"What are you making anyway?" I ask. "One of Ryan's favorite dinners?"

She looks up at me again as she grabs more ingredients off the counter. "Oh no, honey. I'm loading you up on food."

I furrow my brows, having no ideas what she's talking about. "What? Why?"

"Well, ginger rice is good for nausea. Hard boiled eggs supposedly are too. I'm not convinced, but you need the protein anyway. This way you can chop one up real quick with this little device I got you." She rifles around in a plastic sack for a second and pulls out a box with what looks like a vegetable chopper in it. "Here. It'll make the egg really small, so you don't have to chew much. Maybe that will trick your brain and help you stomach it."

I shake my head. "Wait, stop. I'm confused. You're making me pregnancy food?"

"Of course, I am." God love her, she looks genuinely shocked that I would question the whys of this whole scenario. "Honey, you are my daughter-in-law, and you are carrying my grandchild. This is the least I can do to help you out. I wish I could do more."

"Denise, you don't have to do this."

"I don't have to, but I want to. What did we just talk about? We love you and want to support you. When Rowen is home, he can do this. But he's on the road right now and won't be back until we're gone. This just takes one thing off your plate, so you can rest more."

"Well, thank you."

"Really, it's my pleasure. I like cooking. I'm also going to make you some chicken noodle soup. I'll freeze some of it for later. But if you're feeling well enough, it'll have lots of protein. If you feel terrible, just sip on the broth." She picks up a whisk and begins mixing some sort of dough. "And these are going to be gingersnaps. I don't know if you have a sweet tooth, but they still might work better than just plain crackers. At least they'll be tastier."

"I can't believe I'm saying this, but just the smells may have brought some of my appetite back."

Denise looks genuinely pleased with this assessment. "Good. In about ten minutes, it'll be ready for you."

She wasn't kidding when she said she was creating a tribe around us. And it comes with food I can stomach. I'll call that a win all the way around.

CHAPTER 12

Rowen

osing in San Jose is not something any of us anticipated. They're a strong team, but we're stronger. Or at least we thought we were. That is, until Santos didn't show up for our trip.

No one knows where he went. Last I saw him, we were talking in the locker room about nausea and hormones. Then suddenly, he disappeared.

When someone finally asked Coach about it during warm-ups, all he said was, "He's not here but you are. Do your job and focus on the task at hand!"

We all shut up and went through the motions of warm-ups. And then it all fell apart.

Logan has proven himself to be a great back-up goalie, but he wasn't prepared to jump in at the last second because of an injury to our second stringer. That was his own damn fault. It's not like we don't train enough. But the last minute change got into Logan's head, and he couldn't keep the ball out of the net.

That's how the ricochet effect began. I couldn't seem to block for shit. Daniel kept kicking too wide. The stress of the change, and probably more so the curiosity about what was wrong with Santos, just killed our stride. Even Luca Montoya, who is usually one of our more reserved players, pulled a yellow card and had to rein in his defense so he didn't get tossed out.

It was brutal.

So while the Earthquake fans are celebrating loudly in the stands, the Texas Mutiny is walking off the field, with our tails tucked firmly between our legs. Not just in shame, but possibly in anticipation of our asses being handed to us by Coach once we hit the locker room.

"Dude. Where the fuck is Santos?" Christian bellows, arms thrown up in exasperation as Daniel and I meet him in the middle of the field. No one else is sticking around, content to put this behind them as quickly as possible.

"He quit."

Christian and I freeze, stunned by Daniel's admission.

"Wait." We jog to catch up to our captain, trying to decide if he's telling us the truth or not. Because that is random. "What do you mean he quit?" Christian asks, which means I don't have to.

Daniel stops and turns to face us, not wanting to get anyone else's attention. Coach will tell us when he's good and ready, but obviously Daniel isn't thrilled about sitting on this knowledge.

"Just what I said. Went into Coach's office after practice

yesterday and told him he was done, effectively immediately."

"Holy shit."

"Is he okay?" My mind immediately goes to worst-case scenario. Santos loves his job. There's no way he just snapped. "Nothing happened to one of his kids, did it?"

Daniel shakes his head and wipes his brow with his sleeve. "Not as far as I know. Apparently, he had some sort of come-to-Jesus moment and needed to change his life. I didn't ask any details. I just know Coach is still trying to convince him to change his mind, which is why he hasn't announced anything yet. That means you two better keep your mouths shut."

I nod my agreement, but Christian is clearly too pissed off to care. "That's a dick move. The season already started. We can't get Logan up to par that fast. Obviously." He gestures to the field around us, reminding us once again of how terrible we played.

Daniel immediately goes back into captain mode. "Dick move or not, we have a job to do and today we didn't do it. None of us did."

Christian rolls his eyes and they keep half-arguing, half-discussing why the hell Santos left so suddenly. But the more they talk about it, the more I realized I'm not really that surprised. I was there when he and Tiffany were talking at the Funderling's going-away party. Maybe he finally decided it was time to man up and put someone else besides himself first.

Lifting the hem of my jersey to wipe my forehead, I admit, "Maybe I'm not as surprised as I should be."

My two best teammates look at me expectantly, so I continue.

"He's never been the same since his divorce. And I get it. I love soccer. Playing is like breathing. It's under my skin, ya know?" They both nod in understanding. "But if Tiffany gave me an ultimatum"—I shrug and put my hands on my hips—"I don't know. If the choice was soccer or them, I'd have to pick my family."

Daniel seems to understand where I'm coming from. "You're probably right. I'd probably do the same thing if I had to choose between Quincy and the game."

Christian holds his hand up to halt the conversation. "Wait. Back up. Did you just say *them*, Rookie?"

My eyes widen slightly at the realization I screwed up, but I pull it together quickly. I think. "You know I'm not a rookie anymore, right?" I say, trying to distract him.

"We'll talk about that later. And stop trying to change the subject. You just said *them*."

I know I should be going into denial mode. Tiffany and I agreed not to tell anyone yet. But considering how hot my face feels, I'm sure I'm blushing, which they know is a dead give-away.

"Rowen?" Daniel states more than asks as the two of them invade my personal space. I look around to make sure no one is listening in. "Did you knock up your wife?"

Christian chuckles while I shove Daniel playfully. "Shut up, man. That's crude."

"But it's true?"

I try not to grin, but it's useless. Screw it. My lips quirk up in a half smile and I answer quietly. "Yeah."

"Hey!" they both yell and start patting me on the back and grabbing me around the neck. I'm sure if anyone is noticing our interaction, they'd be wondering why we're suddenly celebrating after being slaughtered moments ago. But I don't care. They're excited for me. For *us*.

"You sure didn't take long, did ya, Rookie?" Christian

jabs as he squeezes my shoulder.

"Still not a rookie, Sanchez."

He looks up and taps his finger to his lips, like he's thinking about an alternative. Oh geez. Here we go.

"How about I call you Red?"

I furrow my brow and shake my head.

"Beanie?"

Shoving him away while he laughs, I ask, "How about just Rowen?"

"Nah," Daniel tosses out. "I'm gonna start calling you Baby Daddy."

Christian laughs and puts me in a headlock again, his go-to move whenever he's really excited. After a few seconds, though, the real inquisition begins.

"Seriously, though," Daniel asks as we cross the field, "when is the bambino getting here?"

"Due date is August sixteenth," I say with pride. It feels good to finally be talking about this with my friends. I've only kept it a secret for a few weeks, but this is the most exciting thing to happen to me, well, ever.

"Is Tiffany happy?"

I have to think about how to answer that one for a second. I'm not really sure. Not because I think there's anything wrong with her emotional well-being or anything. Just because it was such a complete surprise.

"I wouldn't say she's happy. She's too busy throwing up. All the time. Hard to feel anything but frustration, I think."

They both grimace, which they deserve. She gets sick often enough, I'm past the grossed-out stage.

But in true Daniel fashion, he has to toss out some suggestions. "Has she tried plain crackers and ginger ale?"

"Yeah. She can't hold it down."

"What about ginger candy? You can get it at all those maternity clothes stores."

Christian confused look makes me laugh when I answer.

"Yep. She hates them. They gross her out."

"Sniffing a lemon?"

"Helps. But not much."

He throws his hands up. "Well, I'm out of ideas."

"Dude, how the fuck did you have so many to begin with?" Christian asks, truly stumped by all Daniel's random knowledge.

Daniel returns the look with one of his own. Only his says *duh*. "Did you forget how many sisters I have?"

"Ah," Christian and I respond in unison.

Putting my hand out, I stop us from getting any closer to our teammates. "Guys, really. Please keep this under wraps. Tiffany is still kind of skittish about unnecessary attention, and I want this to be as stress free as possible for her."

"Say no more," Christian responds, holding his hand up while Daniel pretends to zip his lips closed. "Your secret is safe with us."

Call me paranoid, but somehow, I doubt that.

CHAPTER 13

Tiffany

I KNEW YOU WERE PREGNANT!

Quincy's text comes in shouty capitals, making me roll my eyes at her excitement. My response will probably make her roll her eyes right back at me, only it'll be in exasperation.

Me: *I swear to God those guys gossip more than a bunch of old ladies at church!*

Quincy: *Oh, come on. Did you really expect Rowen to keep it from them for long?*

She has a point. He's been way more excited than I ever anticipated. He even cried when my blood tests came back and the doctor told us it's a boy.

I've never seen Rowen get teary-eyed over anything, but the thought of being a father has him a blubbering mess. It's actually really sexy.

Me: *Touché. Just keep in under wraps for now. I don't want my job to know yet. You know how sticky it can be.*

Quincy: *Yep. It wasn't that long ago I was trying to sort it all out with Chance. My lips are sealed. Wait… I'll seal them after this: CONGRATULATIONS!!!!*

Tucking my cell into my back pocket, I pull open the door into the newsroom. Like usual, Caleb is alone at the assignments desk, most everyone else is out in the field. Also, like usual, I feel like shit.

"Hey Tiffany," he greets without looking up from his monitor.

"Hey." I grab my mail out of my box, preparing myself to climb the stairs to the sports office. I really need to sit down after walking from the parking lot.

Just as I turn to make the trek, Caleb calls out.

"Hey, Tiff, when you get a chance, can I talk to you for a second?"

"Sure. Does it have to be now? I really need to get started on tonight's show." And I really need to sit down, but I don't say that part. Not that I need to. A quizzical look crosses his face.

"Are you okay?"

"Yeah. Fine."

Cocking his head, I have a feeling he doesn't believe me.

"You haven't been yourself since that stomach bug ran through the office. Maybe you need to go see your doctor or something."

I want to laugh because I've seen my doctor a couple times already. Sweet Caleb hasn't put two-and-two together. I'm surprised, and yet not all that shocked. I guess if you've never dealt with a pregnancy before, the symptoms aren't glaringly obvious.

"I'll do that. Thanks, Caleb. Just give me a bit to get settled, and then I'm all yours."

He turns back to his scanners, and I turn back to the stairs. Who knew one flight could be so tiring? At this point, the only thing motivating me to keep going is the thought of the gingersnaps in my bag. Denise was right. They are much tastier than saltines and do a better job of holding my nausea at bay. I really, really want to eat a cookie.

Finally, after what feels like hours, I plop my ass down in my chair, dropping all my belongings at my feet.

Steve chuckles and smiles at me. "Pregnancy is still going well, I see."

"I feel like I've been run over by a bus."

"Close," he retorts. "Just having the life sucked out of you by an alien life force."

He's not wrong. Grabbing my bag from the floor, I dig around to find my treats. "Anything exciting happening here? It's just regular games tonight, right?"

"Yep. No specials stories or anything." He clears his throat. Odd. I'm getting the vibe that something else is going on. "But, uh, there is something exciting happening."

Intrigued and just a little nervous, I stop my digging. "Wha-what is it?"

"I got the job."

My jaw drops, and my bag falls to the floor as I stare at Steve. He's smirking, but I can tell he's enjoying my reaction and is trying very hard to contain his own excitement.

"You got the job," I say quietly.

He nods. "I got the job."

"You're going to New York?" That's the only job I know about, but I still want to clarify.

"I'm going to New York."

Pushing out of my chair, I stand. "Steve, you got a job in NEW YORK CITY!" I shout, barely able to contain my excitement.

"Nailed it!" he yells, but I'm too overcome with excitement to call him out on the weird catch phrase.

As he stands too, a sudden burst of energy launches me into his arms, hugging him tightly. I'm so proud of him. He's been a great boss, but he's also a damn good producer and deserves this.

Releasing him, I collapse back in my chair, barely noticing the exhaustion anymore.

"When are you going? How is this working?" Adrenaline still runs through me, but there is also a lot to plan with this change.

"Well, I'm going to head northeast early to get started working and begin house-hunting. Meg is going to stay here with the girls until the house sells."

"Makes sense. How soon until you leave?"

"I turned in my two-week notice yesterday."

Another jaw drop. "Before telling me?"

I'm not sure if I'm hurt or completely understand why he didn't want to wait. Either way, he shrugs like it's no big deal.

"It was your day off. I figured you were taking a nap."

Oddly enough, I believe that it's exactly what he thought.

I wish he was right. I'm still regretting my decision to spend hours in the car with my in-laws. Admittedly, though, the food was a nice consolation.

"The job opening has already been posted," he continues. "But I gave them a heads-up that you will be putting in your résumé, and I want you to be the front-runner. Unsurprisingly, they acted like I was ridiculous for even suggesting you wouldn't be."

"Or they acted like you were ridiculous for thinking your opinion matters."

He waves me off dismissively. "Regardless, it's already been discussed, and until they give you the official title, you my dear are the interim sports producer."

The magnitude hits me like a shock wave. Interim Sports Producer in the Houston news market at the ripe old age of twenty-four. It's unheard of for anyone, especially a woman. Pride sweeps through me. Even if they don't choose me, even if I'm only the interim for a short while, I'm going to take this opportunity to kick some serious ass. Assuming this baby doesn't kick my ass first.

Steve isn't done, though. "In the meantime, that means we need to train someone for your job."

This presents more of a problem. We could use Manny temporarily. He's the sports anchor, so he's used to writing his own copy. But who would man the booth two days a week when I'm off? Or would I even get time off for a while? I'm running on empty as it is.

A quick rap on the door has me looking up and discovering Steve is one step ahead of me.

Gesturing to the person standing in the entrance, he says, "Meet your interim associate producer."

"Caleb?"

Caleb digs his hands in his pockets, steps through the threshold, and flashes a sheepish grin. "Told ya I needed to talk to you."

I'm sure they both can tell I'm stunned from the expression I assume I'm sporting. "How did I not know you wanted to move into the sports department?"

He shrugs shyly, which is weird. Caleb isn't shy. Assertive. Commanding. Maybe a touch demanding. But not shy. This is a new side to him. "I don't really talk about it. It's always been a pipe dream, but I only have a two-year degree and not in journalism. You know how infrequently these jobs come along. Last time, it was your turn for it to drop in your lap. This time, it's mine."

He's right. The only reason I got this job when I graduated from college was because they were impressed with my internship and were scrambling to fill a sudden opening. It was a case of "right place, right time." I've always been grateful for it because it meant I skipped years' worth of clawing my way to the top. So I understand why he seems unsure. I'm sure it feels surreal to be this close to the beginning of his dream.

Swiveling my chair to look at Steve, I say, "Maybe I'm more surprised that you *did* know."

"What? I talk to people."

"You don't talk to any people except the ones in this office."

"Or maybe I just don't talk to anyone when you're around."

"Clearly." I swivel my chair back around to face Caleb again. Now that the excitement is wearing off, I need that gingersnap. Grabbing my bag, the search is on again. "I guess this means I have two weeks to get you trained, huh?"

A genuine smile crosses Caleb's face, and I know he's already starting to feel comfortable. "Where do we start?"

"Let's start pulling b-roll from last night's games," I instruct, finally finding my cookies and pulling them out of my bag victoriously. "Then we'll work on some copy."

Caleb pulls up a chair to watch how I find our clips and catches on quickly. Pretty soon, we're working in tandem to get everything done.

More than once, I look up to catch Steve watching us, smiling. It feels good to know he's confident he's leaving this office in capable hands, so he can leave to reach his lifelong dream. I won't let him down.

CHAPTER 14

Rowen

Practice was a bitch today. We're finally starting to gel again after Santos's sudden departure, but it hasn't been without growing pains. Our record has dropped into the shitter, but hopefully, we can pull it together for play-offs. The season is long enough, so we have time.

Kicking the door shut behind me, I drop my bags on the floor and head straight for the kitchen. Tiffany drank most of the broth to my mom's chicken noodle soup—it's the only thing she can really hold down, and even then, not always—but that leaves all the hearty stuff for me to eat. With as hungry as I am after practice, none of it is going to waste.

Popping the Tupperware of leftovers in the microwave, I thank my lucky stars my parents are moving here. Yeah, we have separate lives, but if I know one thing, they'll implement family dinners once a week. That means home cooking for this growing boy.

Grabbing my bag, I head into the bedroom while I wait for my food to heat up. I need to get some laundry done so I might as well throw a load in the washer now.

A groan from the master bath stops my train of thought. Instinctively I know something's not right.

Sure enough, as soon as the room comes into view so does my worst nightmare.

"Tiffany!" I yell and race toward her limp form, lying on the floor next to the toilet. "Babe. Baby, are you okay?" I gently shake her, not knowing if she's injured or sick. The last time we texted was just a few hours ago. I thought she was at work.

She grabs onto me, fisting my shirt in her hand. "I don't feel good, Rowen." I take that as a decent sign. At least she's coherent. Until suddenly her eyes fly open and she sits straight up. "Move, move move..." she demands, pushing me out of the way and sticking her head in the toilet to throw up. Nothing happens, though. She coughs and gags and cries, but her stomach is officially empty of anything. Not even bile. That's not good.

Making an executive decision, I race into the bedroom and dump out my practice bag, tossing a couple T-shirts, sweats, and yoga pants in it. Then I grab the bag of toiletries I always keep packed for road trips and throw it in with everything else, just in case we need it.

Satisfied I've got the basics packed, I head back to my wife. "Babe." I gently push her hair out of her face. "Babe, we're going to the hospital."

"No." Her voice sounds weak and small, which cements my decision, whether she wants to or not. "I don't want to go to the hospital."

"Too bad. You are way too sick. This isn't good for you, and it isn't good for the baby."

I think she's going to resist again, but she surprises me when she nods and tries to push off the floor. Wrapping my arms around her waist, I'm careful not to put too much pressure on her stomach. My hand, of course, drifts down to the small bump below, and I say a silent prayer for his protection. I'm terrified for him. For both of them.

"Let me grab some stuff," Tiffany says and tries to pull away.

"Already done. Hold on, babe. You can't walk." Shuffling us over to the where the bag is, I pick it up. Once it's securely dangling from my arm, I wrap my arm under her knees and pick her up.

She smiles weakly. "I can walk, you know."

"Not quickly and not without stopping to throw up," I banter back. "If you're not at work, that tells me you've been sick for at least a few hours. I'm not waiting for you to prove your independence."

She snuggles into my chest and doesn't fight me on it. She knows I respect her, but she also knows I'm right about how sick she is. Once again, I'm reminded of how urgent the situation really is when she doesn't continue to argue.

It takes a few minutes to get the door locked and get settled in the car. A couple of our neighbors looked at us quizzically as I carried her by, but fortunately no one said anything. I don't have the time or patience to talk to anyone right now. My entire body feels wired from the adrenaline racing through me.

The twenty-minute drive to the hospital feels like it takes hours, and I don't think my hand ever moves from her thigh.

Like touching her will somehow keep her from getting worse. Or maybe it just keeps me grounded. Either way, I've never been more thankful for valet parking in my life.

"Do you need us to get a wheelchair, sir?" The valet must see the frantic look on my face because he doesn't even greet me before offering.

"No. I'm going to carry her. Thanks."

Tossing my keys to him, I quickly walk around the car. The passenger side door has already been opened. That's the benefit of having a women's hospital in Houston. Valet is not surprised to see frantic dads and moms in labor. They all work together to get us inside as quickly as possible.

"Come on, baby," I say quietly, hooking my arms under her and pulling her close to me.

The automatic doors open, and I barely notice a rush of cool air that would normally make me shiver. Apparently, the triage nurse has already been tipped off that we're on our way because she gestures for me to follow her straight to the back.

The small room only has a curtain for a door, but I don't care. It has a bed and monitors. That's all I care about.

"How far along are you?"

"Twenty weeks, two days," I answer before Tiffany can even open her mouth.

"Over the halfway mark. That's great! Let's get your blood pressure, okay?" the nurse says gently, placing the cuff around Tiffany's arm.

After determining Tiffany's blood pressure is within normal ranges and there's no fever, she rubs the doppler all over her stomach. I didn't realize I was holding my breath until I let it go in relief when I hear the familiar *thrumb thrumb* of his heartbeat. This is good. This is very good.

"I know this is a bedpan," the nurse jokes, handing the plastic bowl to me. "But around here we use them for morning sickness. Keep it handy just in case you need it. The doctor will be here in just a couple of minutes. My name is Karen, if you need me."

Karen leaves and I collapse into the chair next to the bed, pulling it forward where I can hold hands with my wife.

"How are you feeling?"

"Like shit."

I chuckle, glad she hasn't totally lost her feisty nature. Stroking back her hair, I can't help but feel relief that we're here and she's going to be taken care of. "I probably should have asked this before, but did you call in sick? Do I need to call Caleb?"

She shakes her head gently. "I already called. There's no way I'm getting this promotion Rowen. Not now."

"Hey. You don't know that. Your interview went great."

"Yeah, until the end of it when I finally told them I'm pregnant." She rolls onto her back and rests her hand on her forehead. "Steve left almost a month ago. I'm sure they've offered it to someone else by now."

"Or something more pressing came up, and they know you have everything under control."

She sighs and rolls back toward me, placing her hand on her stomach and rubbing absentmindedly. "Maybe."

"Is he moving?" I ask, gesturing toward her mid-section.

She looks up at me and smiles. "A little. Pretty soon, you'll be able to feel him too."

Before I can respond, the doctor walks through the curtain. She's a petite woman with a short brown bob. I can already tell she's mild-mannered. Probably comes in handy when working with dads like me.

"Hi Tiffany. I'm Dr. Braden, but you can call me Felicity." Turning to me, she puts out her hand. "I assume you're Dad?"

"Yeah. Yes. Rowen." I stand and shake her hand quickly, ready for her to hurry up and examine my wife.

"It's nice to meet both of you. Looks like you're not feeling well," she states, as she looks through information Karen put into Tiffany's medical records.

"I haven't stopped throwing up in about, oh, thirteen weeks or so," Tiffany complains. "So yeah. I think your assessment is accurate."

"Pregnancy will do that sometimes," Felicity responds, typing in Tiffany's responses. "Sounds like you're one of the unlucky ones." Swiveling her chair, she pushes the cart with the computer out of the way and rolls an ultrasound machine in its place. "I can tell just by looking at you that you are definitely dehydrated. That's not good for you or the baby. I'm going to have Karen come back in and set you up with some IV fluids—oh!" she startles as the curtain opens again and the nurse walks in. "Looks like Karen read my mind. Let's give her a one-liter bolus of LR and run it at two hundred cc's per hour after that."

"Got it right here," Karen responds and gets to work setting up the IV. Dr. Braden, on the other hand, has Tiffany shift on the table and lift her shirt so she can squirt warm gel on her stomach. The two of them work in tandem and it's clear they do this enough it's become almost like a dance to them.

In what seems like just seconds, the IV is set up, the lights are dimmed, and our baby is getting his picture taken again.

"Oh! He's big now!" Tiffany exclaims. Already she seems to be perking up and the IV has been in for only a minute. This is good.

"Yes, it's amazing how our babies can look like a tiny little jelly bean one day and suddenly, they look like a real human." Dr. Braden responds quietly, then gets back to her concentration. She takes several measurements and moves the wand to look around at different angles. My eyes never leave the screen, knowing I won't be seeing my boy again like this for at least a few more weeks.

Finally, she shuts off the machine and turns the lights on. Turning to wash her hands, she remarks, "The baby looks just fine. Measures where he should. No sign of a placental abruption. I'd like to do a quick pelvic though, just to make sure you aren't dilating. Is that okay?"

"Sure."

"It's up to you if we get you a gown or if you just shimmy out of your pants."

Tiffany begins to sit up, hooking her fingers in her waistband, but she struggles with the movement. She may be feeling a little better, but her energy is still almost non-existent.

"Hang on, babe." I stop her and encourage her to lie back down, then hook my own fingers in her pants and whisk them down faster than she can.

"Ohmygod, I'm so embarrassed," Tiffany mumbles from behind her hands. Dr. Braden, on the other hand, is laughing lightly.

"Don't be embarrassed on my account. I know how the birds and bees work. You're here for a reason."

I sit down beside her again, holding Tiffany's hand while the doctor snaps on some gloves and makes quick work of her exam. "Nope. No dilation. No effacing. This is all good news."

Snapping the gloves back off she tosses them in the trash and washes her hands for a second time in as many minutes. I admit, I'm impressed with how quickly this is all happening.

"Here's what I think we have."

Squeezing my wife's hand, I brace myself for whatever Dr. Braden's about to tell us.

She crosses her arms and leans against the counter. That's a good sign, right? Not hovering?

"My best guess is you have a pretty bad case of hyperemesis gravidarum. In a nutshell, you are one of the unlucky few that has morning sickness long after your first trimester is over."

"Okay," I say quickly, because this isn't news to us. We've been dealing with it for weeks. "How do we fix it?"

"That's the bad part. You can't. You have to let it run its course. Sometimes it'll clear up. Sometimes it won't. Every pregnancy is different."

I don't have to look to know Tiffany's face just fell. She's been looking forward to feeling better, and it seems like it's never going to end.

"The only thing we can do," the doctor continues, "is treat the symptoms. The worst side effect from a medical standpoint is the dehydration. You are going to have to be very, very careful to stay hydrated throughout the day. I don't care what you drink, water, juice, ginger ale, as long as it's non-alcoholic and doesn't have caffeine, it's better than nothing."

"But I can't keep liquid down." Pressing my lips to Tiffany's knuckles, I know the thought of drinking can sometimes make her gag. Knowing she has to power through liquids probably seems daunting.

"You're going to have to find some that work. Even if you are drinking chicken broth all day, every day liquids. Unfortunately, the alternative is an IV drip and bed rest."

Tiffany's head falls back against the pillow in defeat. Bed rest is the last thing she wants. Not with the sports director position on the line. But the doctor isn't done with her instructions.

"I don't think we're going to prescribe an anti-nausea medication right now."

"Why not?" I question. "She can't hold anything down. I'm afraid she's losing weight."

"It's quite possible that she is. But the baby looks great right now, and the side effects of the medication aren't ideal. If we can control the nausea with bland foods and double down our efforts to stay hydrated, it's really the best course of action."

I sigh. Part of me is still discouraged, but I try to remember what it felt like finding Tiffany on the floor of the bathroom. The only thing wrong with her is severe morning sickness. That's much better than what it could have been.

"I know that's not what you wanted to hear," Dr. Braden continues, "but since your doctor is in our network, I'll go ahead and make sure he's aware of what's going on, and he can decide if there is a better course of action. In the meantime"—she pushes off the wall and pats Tiffany on her blanket-clad foot—"we're going to keep you hooked up to that IV for a little bit, so try to rest. We'll get you good and hydrated before you go. And I have a booklet with all kinds of ideas on foods and beverages to try. It comes in handy."

"Thank you, Doctor—"

"Thanks, Felicity—" we say on top of each other as she leaves the room.

Turning to my wife, I kiss her on the forehead. "Well, it's not ideal, but you are both going to be okay. I'm going to focus on that part."

Tiffany chortles quietly. "I suppose there's a silver lining after all."

"That and I get tomorrow off."

She lifts her head off the pillow in surprise. "You do?"

"Of course," I say with a smirk. "You think I'm going to let you take another day off work without me there?"

Lying back down, she snuggles into the covers and yawns. "I'm not taking the day off, Rowen."

"Like hell you aren't. I found you almost unresponsive on the bathroom floor, and you're in the hospital hooked up to an IV. If you think you aren't taking the day off tomorrow, you're crazy. I'll even get Dr. Braden on your case if you buck me on this."

She smiles and snuggles in deeper, leaning her head on my arm. Before she can even respond, she's sleeping soundly.

And I feel like I can breathe again.

CHAPTER 15

Tiffany

Peeling my eyes open, I don't move, instead assessing my body. It's become my normal. I'm pleased to discover warmth, I'm comfortable, I'm nauseous, but what else is new? I'll take a little stomach churning over actually having to run for a bucket anyway.

Overall, though, this isn't terrible. I'm not sure what the doctor put in that IV, but it made a huge difference in how I feel. I was hooked to it for a few hours before they deemed me well enough to go home with the understanding that I take today off at minimum. Tomorrow is still to be determined.

The bed dips next to me, and I roll over to see my husband situating himself against the headboard, long legs stretched out and crossed at the ankles.

"What are you doing here?" I question. Usually, I wake to an empty house because of our opposite schedules. Needless to say I'm surprised to see him casually lounging around. "Shouldn't you be at practice?"

"I took the day off." He grabs the remote off the nightstand and flips the TV on.

Tucking my hands underneath my cheek, I snuggle down a bit. "Since when are professional athletes allowed to take a day off?"

"Since I told Coach my pregnant wife was hospitalized yesterday, and I needed to make sure she's healthy again before we hit the road next week."

The ramifications of that call are not lost on me.

"Shit. I'm gonna start getting some frantic texts from Quincy, aren't I?"

Without even looking at me he replies, "If you don't already have a few, I'd be surprised."

Hoisting myself up slowly, I lean against the headboard next to Rowen, rubbing my stomach. His big hand joins mine, and I know he's wishing he could feel the baby move. Yesterday was hard on Rowen. Yes, I felt like shit, but I could feel the baby moving inside me, so I knew he was okay. Rowen didn't have that luxury, and I can only imagine where his mind went. I don't have to ask to know he was preparing for the worst when he found me. I feel terrible that he had to go through that.

"How are you feeling this morning?" he finally asks quietly, his favorite new TV show playing softly in the background.

I bobble my head indecisively. "Not as bad as yesterday. Not as good as I did six months ago."

He smiles at my retort. "So, feisty and nauseous?"

"That about sums it up."

"Good." He leans away from me then turns back to hand me my favorite Yeti, a red straw sticking out of the top. "Here. Sip."

"What is it?" I ask, complying with his demand.

"Raspberry tea. Caffeine free, of course. The doctor wants you to sip all day, so I picked up a few things after my run earlier. I figured we can try a few different flavors today, decide what your taste buds like and what they don't like, and go from there."

Taking a few sips, I rest the cup on my lap. "This one's not bad."

"Yeah?"

"Yeah. My stomach is rolling a bit, of course, but not enough to make me stop drinking. And I like the flavor."

He nods his approval. "Good. We'll keep that one on the list. And this should help too." He hands me one of his mother's gingersnaps.

A huge grin crosses my face. "Thank you, babe. I seriously love these," I mumble through my nibbles. Small bites are the best way to eat anything these days. "I need her to make me some more of these when she can."

"Already on it. She's whipping up a huge batch today and going to mail them priority tomorrow in between packing."

I can't help but laugh. "You guys are too good to me."

He leans over and kisses me on the top of my head, rubbing his hand on my pooch again. "It's just because we love you."

Settling in, we spend the next little while vegging out. I hate to admit it, but Rowen's right. *FaceOff* is a really interesting show and the designs they come up with are amazing.

"These people are incredible. They're not just artistic, it's like they're woodworkers or something. Except without wood."

"Like they do construction, not just design."

"Exactly. I mean look at that." I point to the screen. "How much muscle does it take to pry that mold open? Oh!" My hands fly over my mouth. "Oh no, don't drop it!" I watch in horror as the mold the contestant has spent hours making falls to the ground and shatters.

Beside me, Rowen makes his own sound of disbelief. "Oh, that's not good."

We watch for the next several minutes, mouths agape, as the contestant frantically alters his costume design plans for a new head piece. It's a good thing I don't normally watch television. I am way too invested in this now.

As we continue to watch, Rowen reaches over and rubs his hand on my belly again. He does that a lot, and I don't mind. Anyone else? Yeah, they can fuck right off. Don't touch my baby bump unless you want to get an earful and maybe a knuckle sandwich. But it's different with Rowen. We're so much like two halves to a whole, it doesn't faze me at all.

This time, though, he feels it when I do.

His head whips over to look down at his hand. "Was that...?" he questions, eyes wide in disbelief.

"I think it was."

Sitting up on his knees and turning his whole body to face me, the flailing contestant is long forgotten. Rowen shifts so he can put both his hands on my bump and waits. He doesn't have to wait long to feel the soft nudge coming from inside me.

Rowen's breath hitches. "Whoa. That's...wow."

Moving his hand with mine, I put it in a different spot and press down harder. Sure enough, our little future athlete takes aim and kicks the right spot.

"Holy shit, Tiffany. That's incredible. Is he… he's really strong, isn't he?"

I belt out a laugh, my husband never moving or taking his eyes off my mid-section. "You remember what you do for a living, right? And what I used to do for fun? He's just practicing his corner shot."

"Yeah he is."

Another soft push and then we wait. And wait. But nothing else happens.

"I think he fell asleep," I remark, glancing back up at the television. The underdog contestant seems to have made a comeback while we were distracted, painting over some sort of latex bald cap and attaching scales. It actually looks super cool.

"Does it always feel like that?" Rowen settles back into his spot but keeps one hand on my stomach.

"Um, it doesn't feel quite the same as it does for you. I guess the best way to describe it is when you have a gas bubble or something running through your intestines. It's like that, except it doesn't hurt at all."

He shakes his head, still trying to wrap his brain around this new turn of events. "I just can't believe he's real, ya know?"

I turn to smile at my husband. I love this side of him… the sensitive, feeling side.

"I mean, he was real before. But now he's *real*." Rubbing his hand down his face, he chuckles lightly. "That doesn't make any sense."

"It makes perfect sense. I felt the same way the first time I felt him kick. It's not that it was fake before. It's just this sudden realization that pregnancy means an actual human growing inside me. Not just morning sickness and peeing a lot."

"That's it exactly. This is our *baby*. He's going to come out with those same legs that are kicking you now."

"I know. It's a surreal experience." Pointing to the nightstand, I say, "Can you pass me another cookie?"

He chuckles again and grabs two, one for each of us. "You really are feeling better today."

I grunt in response. "I hate to admit it, but I think the doctor was right about the hydration thing. The nausea is always there, but if I keep sipping it doesn't get any worse."

With the exception of the whole sickness and hospital thing, it's pretty nice to take a day to ourselves. I've got my favorite guy. I've got my favorite cookies. Our favorite contestant wasn't eliminated and moves on to the next round of competition. There are definitely perks to staying in bed and resting. But, of course, now I want to research this costume designer and see if he won the whole thing and if he's working in Hollywood now. He should be.

Reaching my arm across Rowen's torso, I wiggle my fingers. "Hand me my phone would you, babe?"

He grunts as he twists to get it, trying not to fall off the bed, reaching so far. "Finally going to calm Quincy's mass hysteria?"

I snort a laugh. "Hardly. I'm waiting to see how long it takes her to finally come bang on the door."

"You're terrible," he says with a chuckle.

Flipping through my phone, I ignore the four waiting text messages, but before I open the internet, I realize I have a voicemail. Weird. I wonder if my doctor is following up on yesterday.

Soon enough I realize it's not the doctor. It's something even stranger.

Noticing me making a call, Rowen peels his eyes off the screen. "What's up?"

"I don't know. HR left me a message." Before he can ask another question, she answers.

"HR, this is Naomi."

"Hey, Naomi. This is Tiffany Flanigan. I got your call." Anxiety courses through me. With the way things are going these days, she could be calling about any number of reasons and left me no indication on which one.

"Oh, hi Tiffany!" Her tone turns cheerful. "I'm glad you called back. First thing's first. How are you feeling?"

Rowen looks at me quizzically. I just shrug in response. "Better. Not one hundred percent of course, but I'll be back at work tomorrow."

"No rush. If you need to take another day, that's fine. We can accommodate you."

"Well, thanks. But really, by tomorrow I'm going to be ready to get out from under my husband's thumb."

Naomi laughs, and I smack Rowen's hand away when he pinches my leg.

"As annoying as that can be, I'm glad he's taking care of you. And truly, if you need to take a day off here and there before maternity leave, just let me know."

"I really appreciate that."

"It's no problem at all. Okay!" Naomi exclaims, and I have a feeling we're switching gears. "I know you're wondering why I've called. I'm excited to say we're ready to finalize the open position, and we'd like to officially offer you the sports producer job."

My face must pale because Rowen nudges me and says,

"Babe?" But I'm too busy letting her words sink in. "What?" I finally say.

"It was clear from the beginning that you are the best choice for the job. Not only are you already here and know the way we run things, the staff respects you, and I even got with our web guys just to look into a few things. After the piece you did ended up on the Hart to Heart website, we saw a spike in our own visibility, which was huge for our online sales. You didn't know that part, did you?"

Shaking the stunned off me, I respond quickly. "No. I had no idea. That's amazing."

"Well, we're very impressed with the work you do, and for it to cross over into other departments is remarkable."

I grab Rowen's hand and squeeze. I think he knows what's happening. In fact, I'm pretty sure he knows, but he's just waiting for me to say the words out loud. He has to wait.

Naomi and I spend the next few minutes making plans. Since I'm already an employee, it doesn't change my medical insurance or accrued vacation days, but I do have to go in a few minutes early tomorrow to sign off on my new pay increase. An increase I wasn't expecting but shouldn't be surprised to be getting. That's what happens when you're the boss. You make more money.

I'm the boss.

Talk about things feeling surreal. That's going to take some getting used to.

Finally, we hang up and I sit there staring at my phone, rubbing my thumb over the screen absentmindedly.

"Babe?" Rowen finally asks, waiting for me to tell him.

Looking up into his handsome face, a smile finally breaks free. "I got the job."

"I knew it!" He high fives me, which is as little weird, but

I'll get over it. "I knew they'd see your value! It's effective immediately?"

"Yep." I nod. "And she's calling Caleb right now to offer him my old job."

"Tiff, this is fantastic. Look at you breaking that glass ceiling."

"Right?" I bounce just slightly in my excitement and a wave of nausea rolls through me. Mental note—don't try to jump for joy.

"How do you want to celebrate?"

I don't even have to think about it when I say, "I want to stay right here in this bed with you for the rest of the day."

A surprised and slightly disappointed look crosses his face, but it disappears only a moment later when he realizes there's not a lot I can do comfortably anyway.

"Can I at least order Chinese Food?"

"As long as you get me some ginger rice, it sounds perfect."

He leans over and kisses me sweetly, pulling away to look in my eyes. "I'm really proud of you."

Biting my lip, I try unsuccessfully to stifle my smile. Because I'm proud of me too.

I got the job.

And I have cookies.

Best. Day. Ever.

CHAPTER
16

losing the door behind me, I try not to intrude on the quiet. It's been hell getting back to Houston.

First, our flight was delayed due to weather, then our team bus broke down, so we ended up getting home way later than anticipated. After five days away, everyone was antsy to get home. Maybe antsy is the wrong word. Cranky is more like it.

Glancing at the clock to see it's three-sixteen on the dot, I tiptoe my way to the bedroom. I need a quick shower to wash the travel off me, then I'll be wrapping my body around my wife. Man, I've missed her.

When I cross the threshold into the room, though, I stop. This is not what I expected to find happening in my bedroom, with my wife of all people. My almost six-month-*pregnant* wife.

"Um, what are you doing?" I'm thoroughly confused as to why she's jumping up and down in the middle of the night, one hand holding her belly in place.

"What does it look like I'm doing?" she says through her exertion as one arm raises and lowers.

"It looks like you're doing half-ass jumping jacks."

Stopping her motion, she climbs back on the bed and lies down, eyes closed and groggy sounding. "Still as observant as always."

"Ouch," I respond, not actually hurt from her snark. "Someone's cranky. Did you miss me that much?" Dropping my bag on the floor, I toe off my shoes then climb on top of the covers, careful to keep my sweaty socks off the bed and kiss her hello.

Her hands immediately cup my face as she kisses me back. "Yes, I missed you. And yes, I'm cranky. You would be too, if your body decided to revolt against you *again,* and suddenly you have restless leg syndrome on top of everything else."

Pulling away, I really look at her face and notice her eyes are a little more puffy than normal. The circles underneath them are a little darker. I wouldn't have caught it if she hadn't said anything, or I would have assumed it was more pregnancy exhaustion, but now I can tell she's not sleeping well.

"When did that start?"

"The day after you left." She pecks me one more time and lies back down. "I'll be right on the edge of sleep and my legs just get fidgety. If I get up and do four or five jumping jacks, it stops happening."

Resting my head on my hand, elbow on the bed, I gently caress her bump. "That sucks, babe. I'm sorry. How is the nausea?"

"Better. But I don't want to talk about it."

"Okay," I acquiesce, shifting gears. "How is the job?"

A giant smile crosses her face even while her eyes are still closed. "Awesome."

"Caleb is learning quickly?"

"He's such a good addition, Rowen." She turns her head my direction, animation taking over her face as she talks about her job. "If I'd had any idea he wanted to be in the sports department, I would have been grooming him a long time ago. He's so excited about being a part of it all. I guess that's not really surprising. It's hard not to be excited when there are games on almost all the time." She suddenly goes quiet and swallows slowly, her tell that she's trying not to get sick.

"Do you need something to drink?"

She shakes her head slowly.

"I thought it was better."

"It is better. I'm only throwing up two to three times a day now."

That's down from eight to ten right before we went to the hospital. While it's not perfect, there is definitely improvement.

"What can I do to help?" I whisper, pressing lightly to see if I can feel our son kicking again. He's got a strong kick, but he's also proving to be a bit lazy sometimes. But only when I'm trying to feel his foot, the little shit. Usually he has some sort of dance party in there when she's trying to rest.

"Take a shower and get into bed with me," she whispers back.

Kissing her forehead, I push off the bed to comply. That

was already my plan, so I'm glad to see we're on the same page.

I made quick work of washing, even brushing my teeth in the shower to save time. Focusing on the task at hand doesn't stop me from thinking about how relieved I am to be home. It's getting harder and harder to leave Tiffany behind. Not that I think she needs my help or protection or anything. It's just hard seeing her struggling physically like this. And every day something new or exciting seems to happen.

Last week, it was new ultrasound pictures. This week, restless leg syndrome. I don't want to miss any of it. The good or the bad. Huffing a quiet laugh to myself as I turn off the spray, I know it's only going to get worse once *mo mhac* gets here.

Mo mhac.

My son.

The realness of the situation hits me out of nowhere again, making me stumble on my feet enough that I have to grab the wall. I'm going to be a *dadai*. Shaking my head, I smile at the thought that at times like this I feel a weird sense of joy run through my whole body. It sounds crazy, but it happens every once in a while.

Finally regaining my balance, I dry off. Forget clothes. I'm exhausted. I'm clean. And I need to hold my wife immediately. The drive to get to her after being away so long is almost primal. And not just for sex. Of course, that's on my mind. But my higher reasoning also knows she needs her sleep.

Finally, I get to crawl under the covers with her. Tiffany rolls over and snuggles into me before I even settle. It takes a second to get us both situated comfortably, but then my entire body relaxes into the mattress. I don't truly understand how tired I am until that sweet moment when all my muscles go slack. Almost immediately, my brain shuts off and I begin to fall under…

Jarring back awake, Tiffany is shaking me.

"What's wrong?" I demand, suddenly on high alert.

"It's happening again," she complains, a whiny tone to her voice. I'm not sure I've ever heard her make that sound before, and I've heard a lot of sounds. It must be the restless leg syndrome.

"What can I do?"

She bites her lip and I know she has an idea. "This is going to sound really weird so don't laugh, okay?"

"Okay."

"It's not just my legs that are fidgety. It's like…I think I just need an orgasm or something."

My eyebrows shoot up and all the sudden I'm wide awake. "You're horny?"

She bobbles her head and makes a face. "It's not that exactly, but yeah. I think that'll fix it quick."

Rolling on my side to face her, I'm not complaining. If that's what she needs, I'm game.

Lying back, she shimmies out of her panties, tossing them on the floor, and my body immediately responds.

"I don't need foreplay or anything. Just a quick one is fine." Tiffany grabs my hand and puts it right between her legs.

I groan at the feeling of her. I love touching her here, and from the way she's writhing, I know she loves it too. But before I'm going to make quick work of getting her off, I want to play.

Running my fingers through her soft curls, I spread my first two fingers out to the juncture of her thighs, moving down, then pulling my fingers together come right back up for a quick circle on her clit.

"This is not giving me a quick one, Rowen," Tiffany complains, hips gyrating and making me chuckle.

"I'm enjoying myself," I justify back.

"Enjoy yourself faster."

Jutting one of my fingers inside her and back out, her hips roll, looking for more friction. I immediately comply, adding a second digit and holding them inside her.

"Right there," she breaths. "Please do it right there."

Moving my fingers forward, I find the soft ridges inside her and keep rubbing. Her breath hitches again, and I know I'm touching the right spot.

"Faster," she demands. "Harder. Please, please."

So I do. I fuck her with my fingers, hoping to relieve her body of some of the stress. It doesn't take long before I feel the familiar squeeze inside of her, her loud moan confirming her release.

Her orgasm seems to go on and on, which isn't necessarily unusual. But not with just my fingers. She wasn't kidding when she said she needed to come. Her body is wound tighter than normal.

Finally, she begins to relax and sighs in relief. "Thank you, baby." She pats my arm in appreciation, then drops her hand to the side, completely spent.

As I reach over to kiss her neck, hoping for round two, she rolls away from me and falls asleep before I realize I've just been shut down.

"Tiffany?" I whisper, her soft snore the only response I get.

Rolling onto my back, I stare at the ceiling, pondering this turn of events. I've heard people say once you have kids your sex life falls apart because you're too tired to care anymore. I just didn't know it could happen before the kid was born.

Chuckling to myself, I make a mental note. The next time Tiffany says she's fidgety and needs an orgasm to go the sleep, my fingers will stay firmly intertwined with hers if I plan to get a piece of the action too.

CHAPTER 17

Tiffany

I miss going out. Not to parties or anything special. Just going out in general. To dinner or a concert or Discovery Green to hang out. It's something Rowen and I used to do all the time when our schedules coordinated.

Tonight is a rare night that we're both off work and commitment free, but instead of going anywhere, we're sitting on the couch binge watching *FaceOff*. Again. As much as I enjoy our newest favorite show, I'm restless. We've done this for too many weeks in a row.

Sighing, I lay my head back on the couch and drop my hand onto my now protruding belly. It seems like it took forever to finally start showing, to the point that I was starting to question if there was really a baby in there or not. But there's no hiding it now. Nor do I fit in any of my clothes. I never got to wear my new silk sundress before I grew out of it. Stupid, fucking, giant boobs.

"What's wrong," Rowen asks, tossing another piece of popcorn into his mouth. For a professional athlete, he eats terrible sometimes.

Feeling grumpy about all of the above *and* that he can eat whatever he wants, I spout off all my thoughts. "My clothes don't fit, and I'm bored."

He stops mid bite. "Is that why you're always stealing my sweats now?"

I crinkle my brows. "You're like seventeen feet taller than I am. You think I was wearing them because I enjoy my pant legs dragging behind me?"

"Maybe." I take a piece of popcorn from his bowl. I haven't tried popcorn yet. I wonder if I can eat it successfully? He nudges me with his shoulder. "Let's go to Walmart."

"Why?" I ask, sniffing the treat, still debating whether I should try it. It smells really, *really* good and Rowen shouldn't be carb loading today anyway.

"Because you're bored, and you need pants."

That stops me just before I pop the bite in my mouth. "You think I'm going to find pants that fit at Walmart?"

"Sure, why not?" He shrugs. "They have everything else. Worst case, you can grab some yoga pants, or whatever, so you won't trip while you walk."

I sigh again and drop the kernel back in his bowl, thinking about how exhausted my body feels. As much as I don't want to leave the comfort of this couch, right now the cabin fever I'm feeling is worse.

Making a decision, I roll around like a turtle on my back, until I finally shift the right way and end in a standing position. I ignore the amusement on my husband's face, knowing it'll piss me off if I think about how he let me struggle because it was funny. He better not try to get that on video.

"Let's go, Rookie. Mama needs a new pair of pants."

I stand corrected. Not only does Walmart have an array of comfy yoga pants, they have an entire maternity section. There isn't a lot I would necessarily wear on the regular, but a few things will at least get me through until I can make a trip to a fancy maternity store in the mall. And it sure beats the hell out of the last pair of leggings that fit and a now-too-tight T-shirt I changed into before we left. I couldn't risk the cart running over my pant leg so this was the next best thing.

"We found you some clothes. Is there anything else we need?" Rowen runs his fingers through his bright red hair, and I know he's kicking himself for forgetting his beanie. He seems to forget it a lot lately. I don't know if he's getting comfortable without it or if the heat and humidity have finally gotten to him.

Looking up at the banners dangling from the ceiling, one of them catches my eye.

"Maybe we should run through the baby aisle," I suggest. "We don't need to get anything, but I kind of want to get an idea of what we're going to need."

From the look on his face, I know he likes this idea. Anything related to the baby makes him happy these days.

"Let's go."

Rowen slows his pace, allowing me to keep up with him as I lean on the cart, and we weave our way through the aisles. I've seen the baby section before but never really looked at it closely. It's a small area in the back, but there are so many choices.

"Oh god," I breathe. "We have to decide on one of a billion different car seats?"

Rowen's chuckle sounds strained. "Forget the car seat. Look how many diapers there are."

Following his gaze, I see what he's staring at, and my anxiety cranks up a notch. "Holy shit. I'm gonna need to do some research on this stuff."

"Uh huh," is all Rowen says as we slowly pad through the area, making small comments here and there about how much crap there is for such tiny little humans. Still, it's the diapers that stop me dead in my tracks. Rowen wanders off as I just stare. There are at least six different brands, each with at least six different sizes. There are ones with aloe and ones that are scentless. Diapers that have the word "organic" boldly printed on the front. How can diapers be organic? What does that even mean?

A short conversation Rowen and I had a few weeks ago at the doctor's office comes back to me. There was some article he read about product testing in the waiting room. Maybe he remembers. If I can find him in this maze, I'll ask him.

Wandering around for a second, I finally hear his voice and head that direction. "Babe," I call out as I round the corner, leaving the cart behind me so I don't have to navigate in any further. "I don't know which brand we decided to get. Was it Pampers or…" As soon as I realize who my husband is talking to, I stop dead in my tracks.

Of all the people I expected to run into, Santos and Mariana and their kids are not it. But here they are, the entire DeLaGuajardo family right in front of us, all of us staring at each other in awkward silence. In a defensive move, Rowen immediately reaches for me and tucks me under his arm. I appreciate the gesture because I don't know what to do.

I'm glad to see them together. I know how much Santos loves his family. But I was an active participant in that family breaking apart. It was all in the past, and I've forgiven myself as much as I can, but this is unexpected and, well, uncomfortable.

I brace myself, expecting to be berated or maybe even punched. But Mariana does the last thing I expect her to do. She takes a big breath and says, "Pampers Swaddlers are really good when they're first born. Do you guys have a Sam's Club membership?"

Shock runs through me. Is she having a civil conversation? After everything she went through? Everything I helped put her through? I'm stunned, but I also very much appreciate the gesture.

"Um… no," I sputter quietly.

"I would recommend getting one," she advises. "Diapers are a lot cheaper there, and if it's a boy, the only diapers that hold Theo overnight are the Sam's Club brand."

"Oh. Okay." I don't know how else to respond. Not only am I in disbelief, but I'm so appreciative of the information part of me wants to keep asking questions. Quincy is the only mom I know, and she was never pregnant with Chance. He's her biological nephew, and she didn't get custody of him until he was two months old. The time frame before that is just as lost on her as it is on me.

"So how far along are you?" Mari asks, surprising all of us when she continues the conversation, never once asking whose baby it is. I didn't realize it was a fear for me that she would wonder until this exact moment.

"I, um." Stumbling over my words, I take a deep breath and try to refocus. "I'm twenty-two weeks."

Mari smiles. At me. I'm standing in the baby aisle with my husband, talking to the ex-wife of my former lover. No one is yelling. No one is questioning my baby's paternity. Am I the only one who feels like I'm having an out-of-body experience?

"The last half was always a killer for me. How are you feeling?"

I exhale out a long breath, my hand clutched to Rowen's chest. "I actually really hate being pregnant. I throw up at least three times a day still. And I cry over everything. All the time."

"Pregnancy hormones are the worst. I was a raging lunatic the last three months with Theo."

A tremendous amount of relief pours through me, and I barely notice the men having some sort of silent conversation amongst themselves. I didn't realize how much I need to know everything I'm feeling is normal. "I'm so glad to hear you say that. I feel like I'm going insane most of the time."

"It'll pass. And you look great."

Santos leans his forehead on the top of Mari's head and breathes in, I'm sure trying to control his emotions. The relief he must be feeling is something I'm sure he can't put into words. I'm having a hard time myself. I never thought Mariana would make small talk with me again. Not that I was actively pursuing a friendship with her. But this small gesture shows what a dynamic person she is. That she could extend this kind of courtesy makes me respect her that much more.

In this moment, if someone asked me who I wanted to be like when I grow up, I'd say Mariana DeLaGuajardo. The thought makes me weepy.

"Thank you, Mariana. Coming from you, that means a lot." I wipe tears from my eyes and Rowen squeezes my shoulder. "See?" I laugh and gesture to my face. "I cry over everything."

Marina then does something I never, ever expected. She reaches over to me and pulls me into a hug.

The tears continue to leak as I whisper, "I'm so sorry, Mariana. I'm so sorry. Please forgive me."

She whispers back, "I already did. Now you need to forgive yourself."

I hug her just a little tighter. "I'm assuming you still don't want to be friends."

Mari laughs so lightly I know I'm the only one who hears it. "You're right. But I've forgiven you and I'm okay with being friendly acquaintances when our paths cross."

That's good enough for me. Actually, it's better than good enough for me. It's everything I didn't know I needed.

We finally break apart and all say our goodbyes. As soon as they turn away, Rowen immediately grabs me again and holds me until the last of my tears dry up.

"She's my new role model," I say into his chest. "Someday I'm going to be as strong and caring and compassionate as she is."

He kisses the top of my head. "You already are, babe."

Kissing me again, we backtrack to grab the cart, done with shopping. As antsy I was to get out of the house, now I'm emotionally spent. It's time to get back home and get on with our lives, leaving the last of my ugly past behind us.

CHAPTER 18

Rowen

When my parents asked if we were free today, I thought they meant to come over to their new house, do a little light unpacking, have some dinner. I should have known better.

Instead, I got suckered into unpacking an entire moving van because my dad is too cheap to hire a moving company. I lived with the man and his cheapskate ways for eighteen years. Again, I should have seen it coming.

But I didn't. Now here I stand, holding one end of the world's heaviest couch, while my dad yells at me.

"Lift with your legs, boyo! Turn it more on the side."

"I can't, Da," I argue and try to adjust to get a better grasp on it. "If I turn it more, it'll be upside down."

"Pah! Don't argue. Just turn it."

A huge clap of thunder breaks up our arguing, and we simultaneously glance at the ominous clouds in the sky.

Looking back at me, he tacks on, "And hurry! I don't want me couch rained on." Easy for him to say. At least he's inside the house. It's my ass that is stuck outside and about to get drenched.

Grunting, I do my best to rotate the couch a different way, so it'll slide through the door. It would *just* fit if it weren't for the legs at the bottom. Had we noticed those before, we would have unscrewed them. But we didn't, and now we're stuck.

"Don't blame me. If you would have hired people to do this like a normal sixty-something-year-old man, we wouldn't be in this position."

He grumbles under his breath, probably cursing me or asking our Heavenly Father why He blessed him with such an obstinate child. You never know with my da.

"I'm nowhere near my sixth decade, boyo. I'm still in me prime, and don't ye forget it."

Gesturing to the sky again, I say, "That's great. But we don't have time to discuss your age or abilities. It's starting to sprinkle."

Cursing under his breath, he pulls the couch again and barks out a few more orders. I don't know what we do or how we turn it, but suddenly the entire thing slides easily through the door, making me fall forward as I try to keep the furniture from hitting the ground. Just in time too. I no more than stand up and a deluge of rain falls from the sky.

"That was close," my da says proudly, clapping me on the back. "I guess Mother Nature says it's break time since we can't bring anything else in."

Taking a breather sounds good to me. But my mam seems to have other ideas.

"Well Mother Nature is wrong." She smiles at my dad and raises her eyebrows. "You promised me you'd hang that shelf in our bedroom, remember?"

He groans and curses under his breath again. Seriously. A moving company would have made this a million times easier.

"Yes, *mo ghrá*." He gives her a quick peck on the lips. "I'll do it now."

"After you move this, right?" She points to the couch, still positioned in the middle of the floor, and I swear she bats her eyelashes at him. But that's my mam we were talking about. I refuse to think about it.

"Yes, mo ghrá," Da says gently then turns to yell at me again, like I'm the one who caused all the chaos. "Look alive, Rowen! Your mam wants this in the parlor."

Suppressing a roll of my eyes, I pick up my end and follow him into the living room. Just as I anticipated, it takes about fifteen minutes of situating and re-situating before Mam finally decides where she wants it in the room. Because you know, lighting is everything.

I drop down onto the cushion when my parents finally leave, leaning my head back and close my eyes to rest.

"Tired, Rookie?" The cushion depresses as Tiffany sits down next to me.

I turn to look at her and can't stop touching her. Intertwining our fingers, I complain, "If I had known we were invited over to provide free labor, I would have said we were busy."

"I don't know what you're talking about." Now it's her turn to bat her eyelashes. "I've had a very relaxing day. I've been served ginger ale and my favorite cookies," she says cheerfully. "Chatted with your mother about some renovations she's thinking about doing. Gave her Quincy's number so she can add her name to the client list. It's been lovely."

I make a noise of displeasure at the fact that I'm the only one who got suckered into this. Not that she needed to be lifting boxes anyway. But I'm allowed to be a little cranky after unloading half a moving van with only my old man to help.

Letting her hand go, I rub the huge basketball she has under her shirt and she relaxes into my touch. It's amazing what a few weeks has done to her body. No longer a small pooch, her abdomen is big enough that there is no question she's finally in her last trimester. She's all belly. From behind, you'd never know she was pregnant, but when she turns around, baby is all you see. I love it. But I also have no idea how it's possible she'll get even bigger in the next twelve or so weeks.

"What do you think he's going to look like?" I ask absentmindedly. It's something I've wondered about a lot. The ultrasounds are great, but they only show you so much.

Tiffany leans into the couch sideways and drapes her legs over my lap, getting comfortable. She looks really relaxed like this. Oddly, that night at Walmart seemed to help her tremendously. I don't think either of us realized how much of the DeLaGuajardo's guilt she was still carrying around with her. But ever since that night, she's lighter. Quicker to smile. Like she's free.

As soon as she settles in, I immediately rub up and down her thigh. It's like an involuntary reflex. "I think he's going to look like you," she finally says.

"You do?"

She nods and smiles at me. "He already does. Have you never noticed his profile in the pictures? He definitely has your nose."

"You can't tell that from a blurry black and white shot while he's still inside you."

"I sure as hell can," she argues. "I told your mom about it, and she pulled out your baby book. I think he's going to be your spitting image."

"Hmm. Poor kid."

She punches me in the arm playfully. "Shut up. He's going to be beautiful."

I'd settle for manly or handsome. Maybe has a great bend in his kick. But her assessment will work too.

My dad walks back in the room, heading toward a tool box I didn't notice was on the floor.

"That didn't take long."

"The shelf didn't come with anchors for the wall. What kind of product that's supposed to hang doesn't come with the supplies to make it happen? *Daoine dúr.*"

Tiffany giggles at his bitching. "What did he say?" she whispers.

"He's dropping curses over whoever packed the box."

She giggles again, this time covering her mouth with her hand. I don't get it, but she still thinks it's hilarious when he gets all riled up. We're still new enough in our relationship that we haven't had a bunch of time to get to know my parents as a couple, but I have a feeling holidays are going to be interesting when these two get on a roll.

Da rats around for a few minutes longer until a huge clap of thunder makes him look up. "What the…" Going straight to the window, he looks through the blinds then turns to us, confusion written all over his face. "Is this a hurricane? Is this what the news is always going on about?"

Tiffany barks a laugh and I can't suppress my own laughter. "No, Da. It's a thunderstorm."

"Are ye sure? The rain is goin' sideways."

"Positive."

"How can ye tell?"

I open my mouth to speak, but realize I don't actually know. I haven't been here long enough to experience one. "I think I'm gonna defer to Tiffany because I'm not sure."

"You mean besides by watching the local news?" Da nods at her question, and I can tell he's nervous. Blizzards, high winds, sub-zero temperatures are no big deal. But this has him spooked. Hurricane season is going to be fun with him around. "Let's see," she begins ticking off all the signs on her fingers. "There would be no water or bread at the grocery store, the lines to get gas would be ridiculous, flooding would have already started, power might already be out—"

"*Mo dhia,* it sounds like the apocalypse!" Da exclaims, and now I know for sure he's going to be freaking out during an actual storm.

Tiffany just shrugs it off. "It can get bad. There are a few that have done some big damage. But it's just something you learn to deal with. Like earthquakes in California or tornados in Oklahoma."

"But flooding? Do I need a boat?"

That puts us both in stitches.

"Not unless you like to fish. The flooding is usually contained."

"Usually?"

She bobbles her head like she's trying to figure out how to explain her thoughts. "We had some issues last time, but part of it was Lake Houston hadn't been drudged in decades so there was nowhere for the water to go. For the most part, the infrastructure is designed to flood on purpose."

My dad cocks an eyebrow in disbelief. "Why would they do that?"

"The highways have areas where the roads are really low.

I know you've seen it, Rowen." She turns to address me. "Like over by the Convention Center where the downtown area is kind of above the highway?" I nod; I know exactly where she's talking about. "It's designed for the water to pool in those low points to keep it away from the buildings. Most times it works. When the flood waters go down, there is almost no damage, and we all continue with our lives. Most people don't realize that though, so they get really nervous and think it's worse than it is. I only know because we do a news story about it every single time there's a storm."

I watch my dad's reaction as he absorbs the information. It takes a few minutes, but he finally responds with a grunt before stalking out the room yelling, "Denise! We need to get a boat!" while Tiffany and I dissolve into laughter.

When we finally pull ourselves together, Tiffany says, "You better pray you are out of town next time there is a natural disaster because he is going to be on our doorstep to hunker down at the first sign of a storm in the Gulf."

"Ohmygod, that's like a dozen or so times over a three-month period."

"Yep." She's still wiping tears from her eyes. "And I'll be shocked if he doesn't have the largest hurricane preparedness closet in Houston the next time we come over."

I groan and rub my hands over my face. "You know he isn't going to hire anyone to do it either. He's gonna make me come over and build out attic space or something. I've never wanted to DIY."

Tiffany burst out with, "I should go tell him he needs to be prepared for air rescue too!"

"That is the worst thing you could do for me," I deadpan. "He'll have me out tracking down bungee cords and carabiners because 'ye can't trust those online folks,'" I say in my best imitation of my father.

Still unable to control how funny she thinks this is, Tiffany proclaims, "Ohmygod, I'm so glad your parents moved here. This is gonna be great."

I just shake my head. I'm glad they're here too, but I'm not sure *great* is the right word. I'll decide after that moving van is finally empty and hurricane season is over.

CHAPTER 19

Tiffany

"Would you get away from me?" I bat at Geni's hands, but she bats right back. She's driving me crazy, wanting to rub all over my belly today. "It's fucking annoying when you do that."

"But I want to feel him move," she whines and moves in for the kill again. This time, I don't bother fighting her off. Whatever. If she wants to give me a belly massage, I'll let her. But if she even gets close enough when some pregnancy gas moves in, I'm not warning her in advance, nor am I holding it in. That'll teach her.

Besides, waiting for my opportunity to crop dust her gives me the distraction I need. I love coming to games, but at thirty-weeks pregnant, it's not as fun anymore, even in the box, which I hate. But it's a better choice than in the stands these days. The chairs are uncomfortable; the noise is unbearable; and I've already thrown up once.

We've only gotten through the first half so far. This is going to be a long game.

"Leave her alone, Geni." Quincy pushes her friend back into her seat so she's not practically lying over Quincy's lap to reach me. "Don't you know you're not supposed to touch a pregnant woman without her permission?"

"Since when did she not give permission for people to touch her?"

"Geni!" Quincy cries out in horror at the reference to my past, but I only laugh. Coming from anyone else, I would be offended, but Geni and I have long since gotten over the idea that you have to be sentimental and tender to be girlfriends. Low-ball digs and name calling is the way we like it. She keeps me on my witty toes. Today, though, she wins.

Reaching out my hand for a fist bump, I smile. "I have no response for that. Nicely done."

"You two are weird," Quincy says with a shake of her head, while Geni licks her finger and marks herself an invisible point in the air.

Shifting in my seat to try and take the pressure off my lower back, my newest discomfort, I look down and see my glass is empty of any liquid. I need a refill of my raspberry tea. Rowen mentioned to Daniel it's the only thing I can drink these days and somehow that info ended up getting to the catering company. They've kept it in stock for when I'm able to come, which hasn't been a lot lately.

The games are usually on weekends, and since I'm off Saturdays, theoretically I can be here on those days. But when you're growing a tiny human inside your body, or in my case what I assume is already a toddler, the idea of walking from the parking lot, through the building, into the stadium, up to the box, and then back down again when it's over, is just daunting.

I went for it today. But now I'm seriously considering whether or not I want to waste that precious energy by walking all the way over to the bar and getting another drink.

"Stop looking at your glass like you want to make out with it," Geni spouts off, proving that I am completely oblivious to how observant she really is sometimes. "I'll grab you another one, so your baby-making hips can stay put." Then she pops out of her chair and walks away.

"No really," Quincy says. "You two have the strangest relationship."

"You'd rather us really hate each other's guts?"

Quincy holds up her hand. "Oh no. I like it this way much better. It's just… weird."

"So you've said."

We turn our attention back to the game as the second half begins. Our guys are doing pretty well. It's taken a bit for them gel with the rookie goalie and new defender. The net has been blocked nicely to this point, but it's been close a few times. Bouncing off the goal post is too close for comfort, if you ask me. And the defender's been juked a couple times, but nothing they haven't been able to come back from.

A plate of food is suddenly in my face and Geni startles me for the second time today with her powers of observation.

"How did you know I was hungry?" Taking the plate out of her hand, I eye the munchies in front of me. I'm not sure much of it is going to sit well, but I damn sure am going to try the smoked Monterrey jack cheese cubes. I miss cheese. My mouth is watering just looking at it.

"Aren't pregnant women hungry all the time?" she retorts,

plopping herself back into her own chair and holds her plate out for her and Quincy to share.

Speaking through a nibble of the best cheese I've ever had in my life, I respond, "Probably. I wouldn't know since I'm throwing up all the time."

A sudden roar of the crowd draws our attention away. Very quickly Quincy and Geni are on their feet cheering for the goal Daniel just made. Damn. I missed it. But really, this cheese is so good. I may need to have Rowen stop and get some on his way home tonight.

"Quincy." Panic runs through Geni's voice. "Something's wrong with Tiffany."

I look up, confused, as I continue to eat. "What?"

"They made a goal." She looks at me like I should be following her point. When I don't respond, she continues "You're not jumping up and down or cheering."

I wave her off and grab another bite. "Daniel makes goals all this time. Do you know how long it's been since I've been able to eat something that doesn't make me barf? I'm gonna cheer for this cheese is what I'm gonna do. Except I'm running out. Can you get me some more?"

"You didn't eat anything else."

"I don't want anything else. Cheese. I need cheese."

Geni rolls her eyes but grabs my plate when I hand it to her. She may be my bitchy friend, but she's turning out to be very useful. I haven't had a craving like this since, well, maybe ever.

Once the celebrations on the field die down and Geni returns with more cheese than I could possibly ever eat—okay that's not true; whatever doesn't end up in my belly is going home with me—we settle into our seats again.

"Did you ask her?" I barely register Geni asking Quincy

until the latter grumbles, "No. I haven't gotten around to it."

"What are you waiting for?"

"I don't want to seem intrusive."

"Fine, I'll ask her."

"Ask me what?" I finally interrupt. I may regret encouraging them, but I don't like being whispered around either.

Quincy turns to face me, pushing a stray hair behind her ear and sucking in a deep breath through her nose. I'm immediately on high alert. Somehow, I don't think I'm going to like what she's about to say.

"Is anyone throwing you a baby shower?"

I groan and drop my head to the back of my seat. I change my mind. I prefer them whispering around me if it means not having this conversation.

"I'm going to take that as a no?" she says hopefully.

Turning my head to look at her, I stay leaning back. I don't know if it's the massive amount of dairy I just consumed or the idea of being the center of attention at a party for a bunch of women who don't even like me, but my stomach begins to roll a bit. The only thing stopping me from giving a definitive no is the pleading look on her face. Dammit.

"Why do I have to have a baby shower? I can buy everything on my own."

Not surprisingly, Geni rolls her eyes and Quincy snorts a laugh. "You would be surprised what kinds of crap you don't know you need until you don't have it. I wish I'd had a baby shower, if only so someone would have gifted me a couple boxes of size three diapers. Do you know how long it takes to disinfect a couch when they grow out of size twos and you haven't gone to the store yet? Trust me. These moms will give you stuff you had no idea you were going to need until suddenly you have to go furniture shopping."

I grimace and make a mental note to pick up some Lysol just in case I need it.

"Besides, it'll be fun."

Even Geni can't hide a laugh at that one.

"Fun for who?" I ask, pointing at the heckler to the right of her. "Geni?"

"Oh, I will have *so* much fun being an observer at this shindig." Quincy smacks her leg playfully before turning back to me.

"Ignore her. She's a hot mess. We can make it really small. Just your closest friends and family."

It's my turn to snort a laugh. "That's a lot of effort for you two, me, and my mother-in-law."

"You wouldn't invite your mom?"

"She lives in Tennessee. She can't afford to come."

"Oh." Her face falls temporarily but brightens back up quickly. "What about some of the WAGs?"

I look at her incredulously. "Most of these women hate me, Quincy, remember? They stood around and watched Jessica Funderling beat me up and practically cheered her on. The only reason they leave me alone now is because of you."

Quincy sighs because she knows I'm right. But she's not giving up yet. "But the poker guys' wives. They're okay, right? I bet they'd come. And some people from your job?"

"I work in the sports department," I grumble. "I'm the only woman."

"But there are other departments."

As much as I hate to admit it, she might be right. I get along with the news producers I work with and a couple of the anchors. It might be nice to invite the production assistant, Casey. I don't know that she'd come, but I really respect her and her ability to stand up for what she believes in. Maybe even

Sasha. I haven't seen her for a while since I don't party any-more, but we used to be really close. And Luca's wife, Jose-phine, sent us a small gift after we got married. Maybe some of the poker guys' wives wouldn't be so bad after all.

"Fine," I finally sigh. Quincy immediately squeals and claps her hands together.

"This is going to be so much fun!" she spouts. "I just need to know your nursery theme and a list of who you want me to invite. I follow some really neat boards on Pinterest and have some great game ideas—"

"No games," I interrupt. "Do whatever else you want, but do not make people have to identify the chocolate bar in the diaper or some shit like that."

Geni chokes on her drink at my outburst, spraying liquid everywhere. There's that payback for rubbing my stomach against my will.

Quincy, on the other hand, deflates a little. "Fine. No games. But you promise I have free rein to do whatever else I want?"

"I promise."

Geni leans over Quincy's lap again and pretend-whispers to me. "You know you're going to regret this, right?"

"I already do," I say, and pop another piece of cheese in my mouth.

CHAPTER 20

My wife is such a good sport. But I always knew that. She's supportive and funny and takes no shit. She recognizes when people are hurting and lets their angry words roll off her back. She doesn't offend easily and can whip out one-liners with the best of them. But the one thing she absolutely hates is being the center of attention.

Most people can't tell because of her love of makeup and short shorts and how she walks with an air of confidence. But I see it. I know she'd rather be behind the scenes than front and center. That's how she ended up with the job she has.

It's also how we ended up having a "couples" baby shower. Tiffany thought if all the husbands came, it would take some of the heat off her and we could share the limelight. Instead, my dad has commandeered the back porch and turned it into the men's area. Needless to say, my teammates have all gravitated toward him and his stories of "playing football the real way—when ye used to fall down for an actual injury and not a pansy-ass way to force the other team into a yellow card." His words, not mine. This has left the living room of my parents' new home for the ladies. That completely backfired on my wife in a big way.

Several times I told her we could cancel this whole thing, but she refused, saying Quincy had put a lot of work into it, and it wasn't fair to cancel. Those two have come a long way since they first met.

Right now, she's sitting in a chair in the middle of the room while people watch her open presents. Like I said, if you didn't know her, you'd think she was having the time of her life, but I know her. She's animated and smiling at all the right things, but I know she's uncomfortable, and not just physically. That smile is forced.

Hearing the raucous laughter outside, I push off the wall I've been leaning against as I stare at my wife. As much as I'd rather be here for her, as the daddy-to-be, I probably need to hang with my teammates for a while.

Approaching Tiffany to give her a heads up, she pulls a tiny baby outfit out of a bag. The light blue polo shirt screams nautical, especially since the matching shorts are covered in sailboats. All the women in the room make "Awwwww" sounds. Except for Geni, of course.

"Ugly… ass… sailor outfit," Geni mumbles as she writes.

"You are supposed to be writing down who gave us what," Tiffany quips to her quietly, making sure no one else can hear their exchange. "Not judging the gifts."

"Oh, I'm judging, all right," Geni spouts back. "I'm judging so hard on some of this shit."

"When I saw those little shorts, I just knew it would be perfect for Rowen's son," Josephine says loudly from across the room in her thick whatever accent. She never lost it when they moved here from Portugal many years ago.

Geni's face immediately changes into a saccharine sweet smile, which probably means she's up to no good. "The mommy-to-be just better take pictures and send them to us when Mini-Rowen is wearing it," she says, eliciting several exclamations of approval from the audience. Tiffany is not one of those. No, she's shooting daggers out of her eyes at her friend.

Chuckling at the exchange, I lean down to kiss her on the temple and whisper in her ear, "I'm going to head outside with the guys. Are you okay in here?"

"I'm trapped inside an elephant-themed nightmare." Her tone indicates she's ready to bolt, but the smile on her face doesn't give any of it away.

Thinking quickly back to our conversations, I don't understand why this is a problem. "I thought you wanted elephants for his room theme or whatever that is."

"I said I was thinking about it. I hadn't decided yet," she corrects me. "Quincy took it and ran with it." Looking around the room at the elephant decorations, and wrapping paper, and giant elephant-shaped cake that is going to be really unfortunate to cut open, she adds, "She may have run a little too far."

"I'm gonna tell Quincy you said that," Geni sing-songs happily, clearly enjoying Tiffany's discomfort a little too much.

Tiffany cocks an eyebrow at her. "No, you won't. It would break her heart, and you know it."

"Dammit, you're right," Geni admits. "Besides, watching you squirm is way too fun. I hope this party lasts forever."

"I may be pregnant, but I'm not too fat to kick your ass," Tiffany grumbles.

Geni just laughs. "It's nice that you think that, hooker. But all I'd have to do is sit on the floor. You couldn't bend over to hit me if you tried and your ankles are so swollen, kicking me would feel like a pillow fight."

Tiffany lifts her legs up to look at her feet and sighs. "At least paint my toenails while you're down there, will you? I have no idea what they look like anymore."

Before Geni can respond, Quincy interrupts them, placing another gift on Tiffany's lap, oblivious to the smackdown about to happen in front of her. "Excuse me, Rowen. Ladies, we need to keep this party moving! Open this," she demands.

"That's my cue." I kiss Tiffany on the top of the head this time, and she grumbles something like "Sure. Leave me to this torture," then plasters another smile on her face.

I almost feel bad about leaving her to go be with the guys, but when I step outside, I quickly realize it's almost as bad out here as it is in there. No, there aren't decorations and ugly out-fits, but apparently, my father has become the center of all conversation out here, and there's no telling what he's talking about.

"Hey, boyo!" my dad yells in greeting. "It's about time ye joined us. I'm regaling yer mates with stories of yer child-hood."

I groan, my hand reaching for a beer out of the cooler. My dad has plans to turn the porch into a fancy outdoor kitchen, but for now, we have to "rough it" with beer on ice instead of in a fridge.

"Did you really whip it out in the middle of a co-ed game to pee on the side of the field?" Christian asks, fist to his lips as he tries not to laugh.

"Hey, when you've gotta go, you've gotta go," Daniel retorts, making everyone burst out again.

Rolling my eyes, I lean against the railing. "You guys really believe his stories? I was three, Da. It wasn't exactly scandalous. Everyone else was either doing cartwheels or picking flowers."

"Bah." He waves me off dismissively. "It's always scandalous when yer son whips out his wee peter in front of a crowd."

My friends all laugh, and I just shake my head in amusement. "Where do you think I get it from? Did you tell them the story of how you flashed all those coeds at university when you took off your track pants to run and forgot you only had your tighty-whities on underneath?"

Sammy Marshall practically spits out his beer and immediately starts choking as he laughs. "Seriously?"

"It was only fer a moment," Da argues.

I raise my eyebrow, beer bottle halfway to my mouth. "You were halfway around the track before you realized why a group of college girls were pointing at you, Dadaí."

He waves me off again. "I'm sure they got over it. Campus police called it an honest mistake and let me go."

The crowd erupts in laughter again as we rib each other and tell our most embarrassing team-related stories. Luca almost won the battle of most embarrassing mistake with his game winning point in high school—for the opposing team. But Christian took the cake when he told us about how he snuck up behind his team captain in high school and pantsed him in the cafeteria, only to discover it was his coach. Who happened to be going commando that day. Suddenly, Christian's speed on the field makes sense—three miles a day at a full sprint carrying twenty-pound sandbags for two months will do that to a guy.

I stand back and observe my friends and family as they continue to pass beers around and break apart into smaller conversations. It's nice seeing everyone relaxed with each other. It hasn't been this way in the locker room, maybe ever. But it feels like that's changing. Like there's a better camaraderie happening now that the toxic people whose egos come before their skills are leaving. Sure, there's always going to be a dick or two on any team. But the entire vibe is shifting. I like to think I have something to do with that, but I suspect it's more about Shivel getting canned, which made everyone else second-guess their shitty behavior.

I don't have a chance to think about it much more as Daniel approaches, handing me another beer.

"How's it feel, knowing this is all for you guys?" He settles in next to me, crossing his feet at the ankles and taking a swig of his drink.

I shake my head with disbelief. "I go back and forth between being excited and terrified and waiting to wake up from the dream. It's surreal."

"Kids are like that. I remember when it finally hit me that I was Chance's dad. I know Erik is his birth dad and all that, but we all know how that is."

We both smirk at his comment. Erik showed up in Quincy's life after she got custody of her nephew, claiming paternity and wanting custody after having nothing to do with any of them before that. It took his mother getting involved to make him realize the best thing for Chance was to leave him where he was and take on a co-parenting role of the baby. Geni getting romantically involved with Erik seemed to help too, being that she's Quincy's best friend. The whole thing is odd, but it works for everyone.

"It was just this weird moment when it suddenly hit me that this little boy was looking to me to be his role model, ya know?" Daniel continues. "That it's my job to love him and care for him and teach him how to be a good man. It's awesome, but yeah. Surreal if you think about it too hard." He points his beer at me. "But you're lucky to have your parents here to help. It makes all the difference in the world."

Blowing out a breath, I nod slowly. "I'm sure it will with my mam. My Da? I'm not so sure."

We look over to see him pinning a button on his shirt. I have no idea where it came from, but it has "Grandpa" written in giant letters. And it lights up.

Turning back to Daniel, I add, "He's a little too excited about being a *Daid mór*."

Daniel chuckles at the comment. "My mama used to be the same way. My sister, Erika, would bitch all the time about her showing up with food or baby supplies randomly."

"Yeah? What changed?"

He shrugs nonchalantly. "She had thirteen other grandbabies and ran out of time."

Before I can respond, my dad loudly burst out with "Anyone want to help me build a soccer field in yard out there? *Me garmhac* will be walkin' before ye know it."

Closing my eyes in defeat, I mutter, "I am so screwed."

Daniel just laughs.

CHAPTER 21

Tiffany

"Holy shit!" Caleb exclaims, jumping out of his seat as he watches in disbelief. "Did you see that?"

I should be excited. I should be jumping out of my office chair and cheering. Or at least wobbling out of my chair. A major league grand slam doesn't happen that often, and it came just when it looked like our beloved Astros were going to lose. That makes it even more exciting. For Caleb.

"I saw. That was cool."

"Cool?" He furrows his brow. "Tiffany, they just tied up the game in the ninth."

"I know, Caleb. I saw," I say grumpily and get back to my typing. I'm paying attention to the game; it's just easier for me to put in the major highlights of a story as they're happening, instead of hand writing it or trying to remember as I scroll through the video later.

Caleb drops back into his chair, visibly frustrated by my bad mood. "Geez, you used to love this stuff. What's the matter with you?"

My eyes snap up to his. "Besides being forty-plus weeks pregnant?"

He looks at me like I've lost my mind, which I probably have. I threw up twice this morning, my back aches, I haven't slept more than three hours at a time in over a month, and at this point, I'm pretty sure I'm going to be pregnant for the rest of my life. On top of that, I'm discouraged. At my regular appointment yesterday, my doctor checked to see if I'm dilated.

Nope.

Not one centimeter. No effacement, whatever that means. No thinning, again, whatever that means. Although maybe I'm losing my mucus plug, but he couldn't really tell. There's not one indication that I'm actually going to give birth, and my doctor won't talk induction until next week saying, "Some babies just go a few days longer than others." Yep. I'm just going to be hanging out, looking like I swallowed a giant basketball that likes to have high-kick dance parties every night for the rest of my life.

As if to accentuate my point, little man takes this exact moment to kick me in the bladder.

"Oof!" I call out, doubling over and praying my muscles hold and I don't pee all over myself. If I don't have this baby soon, I'm going to have to buy adult diapers.

Caleb's face immediately changes from irritation to concern. "What's wrong? Are you okay? Is it time?"

Taking a whiff of my lemon to stave off my nausea, which I've done a lot today, I concentrate on calming my irritations as well.

"God, I wish it was. I'm fine." I sigh. "Just irritated and ready to get my body back."

"Okay," he responds, physically relaxing, but still looking concerned. "You sure you're fine? Do you need more tea or something?"

One thing about working in a department full of men—when you're very pregnant, they go out of their way to make sure you're comfortable. It's like they don't know what else to do with you, so they overcompensate the only way they know how. I'd be remiss if I said I didn't take advantage a time or two. Not that they noticed. This time, however, I decide to be good.

"I'm sure." Making a point to add a smile I don't feel so he knows I'm serious, I say, "But the next time we argue over whether men or women are more stubborn, I'm going to remind you that this one," I point to my stomach, "is already three days late with no sign of moving out any time soon."

Caleb smirks. "I'll keep that in mind."

Turning back to the screen, we watch in silence as the out-of-town game goes into the bottom of the ninth inning. Good for the Astros. Bad for me. I'd like to get this story written so we can move on to the next game.

Shit, I *am* grumpy. Wishing for one game at a time isn't like me at all. I've always loved having multiple games happening at once. Keeps things exciting. Rubbing my lower back from the ache I can't get rid of, I realize exciting is relative. Right now, the excitement of lying down in my bed is what gets me through my days. Plus, this low-grade headache is making me insane and having that much noise in the room sounds miserable.

Just as the Indians pinch hitter hits a line drive to center, making it safely to first base, my phone dings with a message.

It's Denise.

Denise: *How are you feeling honey?*

Gotta love my mother-in-law. She's been checking on me every day but is very careful not to be intrusive. I know she's almost as anxious to meet her grandbaby as I am, so I appreciate that for the most part she holds herself back and sticks to one or two texts a day. Unlike her only son who is driving me bat-shit crazy, calling whenever he has a break during practice and swinging by here to check on me. Yes, he brings me food, but I know that's just a cover. What he's really doing is making sure I haven't gone into labor without him. I let it slide because of the ginger cookies.

Me: *Like if your son ever comes near me again, I'll castrate him.*

Probably not the best way of expressing my feelings to my mother-in-law, but at this point, I'm beyond caring.

Almost immediately, my phone rings. Muttering curses under my breath about Rowen checking on me, *again*, I'm pleasantly surprised to see it's Denise.

"Hi Denise." As cranky as I am, I'm glad to have an excuse to close my eyes and rub my forehead. I've had a slight headache for a couple days now.

"Oh honey, you don't sound good."

Wow. My mood must be really bad if she can hear it through the phone.

"Sorry. You're not the first one to tell me I sound cranky today." Caleb looks at me over his shoulder and laughs. I return his laugh with a glare that makes him laugh even harder.

Asshole.

"No, it's not your mood," Denise clarifies. "You just don't sound right. I can't describe it. How are you physically?"

"Eh," I shrug and rest the phone on my shoulder, making it easier to jot down the double that just put the Astros in a really bad position on this game. The bases are loaded at the bottom of the ninth in a tied game. Not good for them at all. "My back is aching. I've thrown up a couple times. Oh, and I can't get rid of this damn headache. It's not horrible, it's just annoying."

"Hmm. Tell me about the backache."

"What about it?"

Done with my notes, I use my free hand to check to make sure the heating pad I'm leaning against is still on and rub the spot at the base of my spine again. So annoying.

"Is it an ache or a sharp pain? Does it come and go?"

I think for a second trying to decide. "I don't really know. I haven't thought about it. I just notice it sometimes. The heating pad was helping for a while, but I'm not sure it's doing much good anymore."

The only response she gives is "hmm," which makes me take notice. Denise isn't a "hmm" kind of person. Usually she comes right out with whatever she's thinking, in her own non-confrontational way.

"What does 'hmm' mean? What are you thinking?"

"Oh, I just wonder if you're having back labor."

Her assessment makes me pause, mid-type. I hadn't thought of that before, but it might make sense. I've been having the pain for a couple of days, and it seems to be getting worse.

"I take it by your silence you're starting to wonder the same thing."

"Yeah. Yeah, I am. But how will I know for sure?"

She laughs lightly, but I don't feel like it's at me. At least I hope not. "Early labor is really hard to detect. Once you're in hard labor, you will absolutely know. Somehow I don't think you're going to get off with an easy delivery."

"Not with the way things have been going," I mutter.

"You have had a rough go of it," she agrees. "I think the other symptoms showing up today combined with the back pain may mean things are starting to happen."

"God, I hope so," I huff out. "I don't know how much more I can take."

"Oh honey, you're going to find out you can take so much more than you realize. Welcome to motherhood."

I grunt my thanks, noncommittally, just before Caleb jumps up from his chair, cheering for a third strike out, moving this game right back into the grasp of his beloved team at the top of the tenth.

"Anyway, I can tell by the cheering that you're busy. I'll let you get back to work. But Tiffany, start trying to figure out if there is a pattern to the back pain. If it spikes and recedes. That type of thing."

"Yeah. Yeah, I will," I agree. "Thanks for mentioning it."

We say our goodbyes and hang up, to carry on with our day. For the next few hours, I pay closer attention to my body, and as it turns out, she's right. For the most part, my back pain is an annoying ache, but about every five minutes, it cranks up a notch to the point where I'm rubbing it. And that's when I need to sniff my lemon the most too.

Unfortunately, by the time the six o'clock newscast is over and we're turning on the Texans preseason game, even the lemon isn't working.

Breathing deeply through my nose, I close my eyes and

hold my hands on my stomach, willing it to calm down. The baby isn't making things any better, though, as he wiggles and moves around. Very quickly, I realize I'm fighting a losing battle. Grabbing my trash can because there's no time to make it to the restroom, I throw up.

And throw up.

And throw up.

There's no way this can get worse. Until it does.

Feeling a gush of water, I realize I'm not only puking in front of Caleb and Mannie, our sports anchor who just made a food run, my bladder finally gave out and I'm peeing all over myself.

Finally, my stomach stops revolting, but my embarrassment remains.

"Tiffany?" Caleb says quietly. "Are you okay?"

Refusing to look at him, I tie the bag of my trash can together, thankful I don't have to go dump puke into the toilet and clean the can out. "I'm more embarrassed right now that I think I have ever been."

"You don't need to be embarrassed. But I think you need to call Rowen."

Glaring up at him and avoiding eye contact with Mannie now, I snark, "Why? So I can tell him I just peed all over the office?"

Caleb's eyebrows rise just slightly.

"Um, Tiffany, I don't think that's pee," Mannie says.

Looking over at him finally, I try to figure out what he's talking about. He gestures to my lap.

"Tiff, I think your water broke."

Assessing how my body feels, I realize, he might be right. A quick Kegel confirms I do, in fact, still need to actually go. Just as quickly as I figure that out, a back spasm hits me so hard, I hiss in a breath and begin kneading my spine.

"Oh yeah. You're definitely in labor," Mannie adds.

"She's in labor." Caleb's face pales. "What do we do?"

Mannie claps him on the shoulder, calming him before the pending freak-out happens. Thank God. That's the last thing I want to deal with. "You get to call maintenance and have them come up here to clean up. Then you get to finish writing the show and take over for her. Sounds good?" Caleb nods and stumbles as he heads to his desk to find the number he needs.

Turning to me, Mannie kneels down, careful to not drop his knees in the fluid. "Do you want me to call Rowen? Or I could call an ambulance. It's whatever you want."

Cocking my head, I eye him critically. "Why are you calm?"

He chuckles lightly. "Before I decided I wanted to be a sports anchor, I was pre-med for a couple years and worked as an overnight orderly for a small hospital. You'd be surprised how many times I've done this."

Well, color me surprised. "How did I not know this about you?"

He shrugs. "It never came up. But it sure comes in handy now. For instance, I know that it's probably going to be at least a couple hours until this baby is born, so there isn't a reason to freak out. But we do need to get going. Who do you want me to call?"

I open my mouth to tell him to call Rowen, but something stops me. He's been on edge this whole pregnancy, and I know he's about to panic. As rude as it sounds, I just don't have it in me to try and calm my husband down while dealing with the physical issues as well. He's going to have to wait.

"Can you hand me my phone? I think the best person to

drive me to the hospital right now is my mother-in-law."

Mannie smiles in understanding. "Yeah, I've seen that a few times too. Probably a smart idea."

Handing me the device, he gets to his feet to talk Caleb off the ledge again and help coordinate the maternity plan HR helped us put in place. Poor guy's hair is already standing on end from running his fingers through it. Tonight's show is going to be interesting, especially behind the scenes.

Taking a moment to center myself before calling Denise, I let it all sink in.

I'm about to have a baby. I wasn't sure I wanted this at the beginning, but suddenly, I'm really excited.

I'm going to be a mom.

CHAPTER 22

When my mam stopped by my place at dinnertime, I thought she was dropping off more food for my wife. I took the opportunity to show her the nursery that was finally complete. Tiffany eventually decided the elephant theme was kind of cute, which made it easier to pick out paint colors and furniture for our former office space. I think it turned out great.

Light gray walls with a white crib and matching dresser, a few stuffed animals and cardboard books ready for when he's old enough to play with them, and a white wooden rocking chair with grey and white striped cushions. It's calm and soothing and ready for my son to grow up in.

My mam agreed it turned out nicely. Then she told me to grab Tiffany's hospital bag because it was time to bring that son into the world.

Needless to say, my first instinct was to race out the front door for my car. It wasn't until I actually got to said car that I realized I didn't have the hospital bag. Or the car keys. Or even shoes. At that point, it made sense to why Mam just showed up instead of calling.

Fortunately, the two most important women in my life conspired against me and decided to pick Tiffany up first, thereby reducing the amount of time I knew she was in labor before making it to the hospital. It was the longest twenty-minute drive of my life, and I'm almost positive I was almost punched in the junk twice for hovering over Tiffany.

In hindsight, I have no idea how they both were so calm, but I guess that's the difference between first-time moms and first-time dads. I literally have no way to gauge what's happening in her body. The baby could fall right out without me realizing it's coming, so that's what I always plan for. She, on the other hand, feels everything and can tell exactly where he is at all times.

Also, I might be a little more like my Da than I realized. They didn't bother to call him at all until Tiffany was safely admitted and settled in. It's a good thing too. We're already eight hours into this endeavor and nothing has happened yet. Well, Tiffany's mom FaceTimed in for a few and Da caused a ruckus in the hall trying to find us. But that's been the most excitement we've had.

I was warned that labor could take a long time. I just had no idea it would be this long.

"Ooooh, not again...." Tiffany groans, and I lean forward to rub her lower back. When we first got here, she tried to lie down nend nap, but her back labor kept her from getting comfortable. For a while, we decided to walk. It helped a bit, but not enough. Now she's trying a birthing ball in the hopes Baby Flanigan will move down a bit and make an appearance.

"A little to the left," she directs, and I move my thumbs where she wants them. We've been at this for eight hours and my wife looks beautiful, but she also looks rough. Her dark hair is up in a messy bun that's got more mess than bun at this point. Remnants of yesterday's makeup are faintly smeared on her sweaty face, even after using wipes to remove as much as possible. She's wearing a black sports bra under the hospital gown and brown hospital socks. I know she feels sweaty and dirty. But mostly she feels pain.

"Ooooh... Stop rubbing," she demands and grabs my hand to squeeze, leaning her head on the rolling table in front of her.

"Breath through it, baby," I say gently. "I got you."

She does as I say, moaning through most of the contraction, and squeezing my fingers as tightly as possible. I hate seeing her like this. Hate seeing her in so much pain that never seems to end. If I could change places with her, I would in a heartbeat. But I can't. The best I can do is try to stay calm and follow her lead. Right now, she wants me behind her, rubbing her lower back while she sits on the ball, so that's what I do.

Eventually, she relaxes a bit.

"Thirty-eight seconds." I have never had more appreciation for my mother than I do now. She's been with us the whole time, timing contractions, while quietly reading her book.

"How far apart was that one?" I ask, wondering once again how long until Tiffany will be out of so much pain and still not totally sure why she is refusing an epidural.

"A little over three minutes. We're getting there."

"Not fast enough," Tiffany groans, and leans back against me.

Wrapping my arms around her waist, I feel her stomach. It's hard as a rock. No wonder she's hurting so badly. Giving her a quick kiss on her neck, I let her relax in my arms, hoping I'm able to give her even a small reprieve from the pain. Just as her breathing begins to slow down like she's dozing off, she sits back up.

"Oooooh… Not again." She grabs both my hands and squeezes tightly, trying to breathe through it. The on-call doctor who has been here all night walks through the door at some point and speaks quietly to my mother, while I whisper what I hope are comforting words to my wife as she powers through yet another contraction.

When she begins to relax, the doctor heads to check the monitor next to the bed.

"How are we doing?" Even though the doctor is kind about it, I know Tiffany is irritated by the question. It's three in the morning and she's been having back contractions less than five minutes apart for the last eight hours. The answer is pretty obvious.

"Like all of my insides are trying to be ripped out of my body."

Making quick work of washing her hands, the doctor grabs some rubber gloves. "Well let's see if we can't get an estimate on how much longer we have, shall we? Can you hop up on this bed for me?"

Tiffany laughs humorlessly. "No. But I can do my best to climb up there."

"Good enough for me."

I help Tiffany get on the bed, taking a break when another contraction hits, and do my best to settle her. I'm exhausted from being up all night, but it's nothing compared to what she's going through. I understand why men in decades past stayed in the waiting rooms during this process. I feel so helpless.

Tiffany tenses and grabs my hand when the doctor puts her hand between her legs to check on her progress. I watch the doctor's face closely, looking for any indication that we're almost done, but what I see isn't encouraging. She doesn't look how I imagine a doctor getting ready to deliver a baby would be. There's no sense of urgency. She doesn't tell the nurse to get more supplies or more people. She just peels her gloves off and washes her hands.

"It's been about eight hours since your water broke, right?"

Tiffany and I nod in unison, both anxious to hear what she has to say. Unfortunately, for us, she sighs in response.

"You're only dilated to about a two right now."

Tiffany's eyes widen. "That's it?"

The doctor nods and crosses her arms as she leans against the counter. "That's it. I know you don't want any drugs if you can help it, but I really think we need to start you on some Pitocin to get things moving. If you were progressing faster, I wouldn't suggest it, but I think your body might need a little bit of help."

Tiffany drops her head back on the pillow, clearly feeling defeated.

Stroking her hair back from her face, I do my best to help comfort her. "Babe, I'm worried about you. I know you don't want to take anything, but you've been at this a long time. I think it's something we need to consider at this point."

She turns to look at me, tears in her eyes. "I'm trying to be a good mom," she says quietly. "I don't want to do this wrong."

Kissing her forehead, my heart hurts for her. I knew she was worried about how she was going to balance it all, but I didn't realize how afraid she is. It makes sense. There have been a mass amount of huge changes in our life in a short time—marriage, her promotion, my parents moving here, a baby. Sometimes it feels like a balancing act of changes when we haven't found our footing in our relationship yet.

Leaning my forehead against hers, I cup her cheek. "You're already the strongest mom I know, just by getting through this pregnancy."

She sniffs and nods. Then turning back to the doctor, she takes a deep breath. "Yeah, okay. But what's going to happen?"

The doctor gestures to our nurse, whose name I also can't remember, and she begins pulling out various tubes and needles while the doctor turns back to us.

"Since you're in labor, the Pitocin is going to just kick it into high gear."

"Higher gear than this?" I ask, not liking the sounds of that.

The doctor smiles kindly at me. I get the feeling she's used to that question. "Right now, her contractions are between three and a half to four minutes apart. We want them closer to two minutes. That should trigger your cervix to start opening up to get ready for baby. Once your labor really gets rolling, we can get you an epidural if you change your mind."

Tiffany shakes her head and watches as the nurse rubs alcohol on the top of her hand, prepping her for the needle. "Let me labor for a little longer. It could go really fast, and then there wouldn't be a need for one, right?"

"Maybe," the doctor says noncommittally. Somehow, I have a feeling she thinks we're in for more long hours. "But we don't have to decide anything right now. Let's just see how this goes."

Tiffany nods, not even jumping when the needle slides smoothly into her skin.

"Let's start pit augmentation and titrate as needed until adequate," the doctor says to the nurse. "We'll see where her contractions are at in the next hour."

The nurse nods and hooks up a bag to the IV pole next to the bed.

"I'll be back to check on you in a bit, okay?"

Tiff nods again, resting back against the pillow with her eyes closed. It's short-lived though. Within seconds, she's squeezing my hand and moaning as another contraction hits.

Another eight hours. Another one centimeter dilated. Almost. I may be rounding up out of my own feeling of desperation. This entire experience is not at all like I expected. Not that I knew what was supposed to happen. Sure, we'd taken a birthing class one Saturday, but that was months ago when our schedules allowed us both to be there. And it never told us what would happen if Tiffany's body refused to do what it should.

At least Tiffany's sleeping now. About four hours after the Pitocin began, she started crying, saying she couldn't do it anymore. She'd been awake for almost twenty-four hours and had been in some form of labor for over half of it. Plus, once the drugs kicked in, her contractions went from being painful to downright excruciating. It didn't take much convincing for her to finally decide to have the epidural. But it did take my Mam physically moving me out of the way to help her through all her fears—fear of a needle in her spine, fear of the drugs hurting the baby, fear of not being strong enough to be a good mom.

That one took me by surprise. It never occurred to me that my wife, the strongest woman I know, would be afraid of being a bad mom. Mam later explained to me that it was a common fear among first time moms and not one I could ever understand. I have no idea what she meant by that, but I suppose it proved her point.

Sitting down next to me on the blue vinyl couch, my father hands me the largest cup of coffee I've ever seen. Eyeing it before taking a sip, I can't help but question him about it. "Where did you get a cup of coffee this size?"

"Starbucks," he responds, like he didn't just say the last thing I expected to hear. "It's the only place ye can get a trente."

I stare at him like he's lost his mind. "How do you know they have trentes?"

"Everyone knows they have trentes."

Maybe it's the exhaustion, but I'm so confused. "You don't like Starbucks, Da. It's a chain and according to you, they help contribute to the rising cost of living and ultimate demise of the state of the economy."

He shrugs like I'm not saying anything he doesn't already know. "I made an exception this time. Figured ye need a bigger caffeine boost than normal and hospital coffee is never good. Did ye get any sleep overnight?"

I lean back next to him and stretch my legs out. My back aches, and I'm beyond exhausted, but, except for closing my eyes, I haven't slept at all.

"I can't. I'm wiped, but it's like this hum running through my body, that's keeping me awake."

"That'd be the adrenaline. Happened to me too, when yer mam gave birth te you."

"Really?" I turn to look at him. We've never really talked about when I was born. I know the basics—my birthday, what city we were in, that kind of thing.

"Of course. Yer mam was radiant before she had ye. Just lovely. She loved being pregnant. Said she never felt better in her life. But then when it was time for ye to get here—scariest day of me life."

"How come?"

He looks at me with sympathy. "I was helpless. It was me job to provide for her and take care of her. But I couldn't take away the pain. I couldn't make it better and I didn't like that."

"Yeah." I nod in understanding. "You know I've been up for over twenty-four hours, not even a nap after practice, and I don't think I could sleep if I tried. I'm afraid of not being coherent if something happens."

Da pats me on the leg in sympathy. He gets it. "I understand, boyo, but yer not going to be good to anyone if ye don't have any rest. Once yer *leanbh* gets here, there won't be any sleeping anymore."

I chuckle slightly and rub my hand down my face. He's right. I know he is. That doesn't mean I can do anything about it. But, of course, my Da has a plan.

"Now that yer mam is at home gettin' some rest, I'll be here with ye for a while. Why don't ye lie down on this lovely couch," he says it sarcastically, running his hand over the vinyl that will probably stick to my skin. "I'll keep an eye on Tiffany. Make sure she's okay. If anything changes or they need ye, I'll wake ye."

There are only two people in the world besides Tiffany and me that I trust with my son's life. They've been taking shifts sitting with us in this room while we trudge through what is arguably the biggest, most life-changing day of our lives. Knowing my Da is here and ready to take over for me, my body suddenly relaxes, and a nap sounds perfect.

"Yeah," I mumble. "Yeah I think I might be able to sleep for a little bit."

Putting my coffee down on the rolling table, my Da hands me the pillow and blanket someone brought in overnight, then pats me on the back and moves to the bedside chair, ready to keep watch over my family.

That picture is the last thing I see as I curl up on the couch and finally shut my eyes.

CHAPTER 23

Tiffany

A low murmuring pulls me from sleep. I know it's only been a couple hours, but I feel so much better than I did. Damn that epidural for being as amazing as everyone said it would be.

Peeling my eyes open, I roll slightly onto my back to see Dr. Hermann and Ryan chatting like old friends. A few seconds of eavesdropping and I finally catch the source of their newfound connection—Ireland. Apparently, Dr. Hermann spent a summer backpacking through Europe and caught a couple games when Ryan was in his prime and playing in front of his hometown fans. I'm sure the tales are tall right now, but at least their relaxed chatter means nothing wrong is happening on my side of the room.

Glancing around, I finally catch sight of my husband who

is sleeping soundly. I'm glad to see him getting some rest. He's been trying so hard to be strong for me. It's not gone unnoticed. But at last count he'd been awake for thirty hours. It was wearing on him.

"Ah, *inion sa dlí,* yer awake."

Ryan steps toward me and kisses me quickly on the forehead. He's never done that before, but I guess I've never been giving birth to his grandchild either.

"How are you feeling, Tiffany?" Dr. Hermann washes his hands and snaps some gloves on. As nice as the overnight doctor was, he's been with me from the beginning, so I'm glad he's here now.

"I'd like to say I feel a little better since I got some sleep, but really it just took the edge off."

He taps my legs, silently telling me to bend my knees so he can check my progress. I've been doing this for eighteen hours. I know the drill at this point.

"Wait!" Ryan exclaims. "Do I need to leave before ye stick yer hand, uh, there?"

I stifle a laugh when Dr. Hermann stops and looks at me to decide. Patting Ryan's arm, I say, "It's okay. Just stand right here at my head and it'll be fine."

Dr. Hermann takes that as his cue to continue with his exam. I don't even flinch this time. That's the one weird thing I've learned about labor. The pain is so intense for so long, nothing else hurts. Not needles. Not people shoving their fingers in your vagina. I could probably have a kidney removed right now and barely feel it. My pain receptors are underwhelmed with anything other than contractions.

From his sigh as he takes off his gloves, I already know he doesn't have good news.

"Just tell me," I blurt out.

"I'm starting to get concerned." Those four little words have my breathing picking up and my heart beating just a little faster. "You've been in labor for over eighteen hours, on Pitocin for ten of it, and you're only a little over three-centimeters dilated."

"But it's working though, right? I'm still moving the right direction?" I feel Ryan's hand on my shoulder as a sense of panic starts to set in.

"Yes, but not fast enough. That and I've been watching your blood pressure begin to rise." He sits on the edge of my bed and I can already tell he's trying to soften the blow of whatever he's about to say. "I know it's not what you wanted, but we really need to start considering a C-section."

No. No, no, no. I don't want a C-section. I'm supposed to have Rowen sitting behind me, helping me hold up my legs while I push our baby out into the world. I'm not supposed to be strapped to a table while he's cut out.

My squeeze my eyes shut, trying hard not to cry. "Do we have to?"

"We're not at a critical level yet," he answers. "The baby isn't in distress. You aren't in distress. But from everything that's happening, your progress appears to be slowing down, not increasing."

I barely notice Ryan leave my side, barely register him saying, "Rowen. Mack, ye need to wake. Yer wife needs ye," until Rowen is suddenly at my side, wide-eyed and looking frantic with his hair sticking up at all ends.

"What's wrong?" he demands.

"Nothin's wrong yet, Mack," Ryan answers. "There's just some decisions to make that ye need te be part of."

Dr. Hermann gives Rowen the rundown while he climbs next to me on the bed and puts his arm around me. They discuss different options while I let the tears flow, hiding my face in the safety of Rowen's shirt. I've been in an extremely vulnerable position for months. It's worse than having people see me cry.

"Tiffany." Rowen rests his forehead on the top of my head, running his hand up and down my arm. "Babe. I think we need to consider this."

A sniff is my only response. I don't know why I'm surprised by this. My entire pregnancy has been one nightmare after another. I should have seen it coming, but I didn't. This is something I didn't plan for and it pisses me off.

I've always subscribed to the belief that it's "my body, my choice" in almost everything. That doesn't just include being pro-choice, it includes my decisions about sex, and my job. I've always been that way. But no one tells you that when you have a baby, sometimes you don't get a choice.

I know Dr. Hermann is letting me weigh the options. I know that if I said no, he'd let me continue on and we'd all pray for a miracle. I know technically it's my choice, but really, it's not. This baby has all the control over my body in this situation, and he's not choosing what I want. It pisses me off that he's taking away my control. And it's pissing me off that I'm blaming him for my misery and he's not even born yet. If this is how I'm going to feel every time he does something that inconveniences me, I'm already on track to be the world's worst mother.

"I feel like I'm failing him," I whisper so no one but Rowen can hear me.

I can practically feel his surprise when he shifts, situating us face-to-face. Thankfully, my doctor and my father-in-law have started chatting again, so Rowen and I can have some privacy. "Tiffany, this is just a change in the play. You of all people know how easily it can happen. I know this isn't soccer, but it's not that different. We go into every match with a plan, but sometimes it doesn't go like we expected. There's an injury or a new goalie." I smirk at his reference to the issues the team had early in the season. "The objective is always the same, but how we get there doesn't matter as long as we do. It's the same thing here. It doesn't matter how he gets here as much as it matters that it happens safely for both of you."

I sniff again, but my tears have all but dried up. "We've been deflected."

He nods and smiles at me. "Exactly. It's a change of play. But in the end, when we're holding him and taking care of him, we'll forget about everything except that we won."

I chuckle lightly. "You realize this is the worst analogy ever."

He smiles back, knowing I'm okay with moving forward now. "But did it work?"

"Yeah. I'm scared though."

He rests his forehead on mine and closes his eyes. "Me too."

Taking a moment to pull myself together, I finally take a deep breath and turn to Dr. Hermann. "Okay. I understand. I really don't want a C-section, but I would rather have a healthy baby even more. Plus, with the way this pregnancy has gone from the beginning, I have no doubt it could get much worse if we aren't conservative with this."

"I really do think you're making the right choice," Dr. Hermann agrees. "I don't like doing C-sections if I can help it. Hell, I didn't want my own son to be born that way. But he was, and he was healthy, and that was all that mattered. I want that for your son too."

"I know." And I do. He's never given me any reason to think otherwise. "What happens now?"

"Now you get to relax." He pats my leg and stands up, presumably to get ready. The nurse who has been monitoring also seems to be moving at a faster pace than before. "First, we're going to check to see if there is an operating room available, but I assume that's already been done?" he asks the nurse.

She nods. "Just did. I have you in OR 3 in thirty minutes."

"Well there ya go." Dr. Hermann smiles like everything is already lining up nicely. "We'll start getting you prepped and in half an hour, we'll roll you into the OR so we can meet your baby."

"I get te go with her, right?" He's been good at covering it, but I know full well Rowen's nerves have just kicked in by the accent bleeding through.

"Absolutely." There's no hesitation at all in Dr. Hermann's words. "We'll get her situated in the OR first while you're getting dressed in scrubs. Then we'll bring you in before we begin. If you have a camera, bring it with you."

Rowen nods, and I can almost hear the cogs turning in his brain. He's nervous and excited, but I know he's feeling as overwhelmed as I am.

"I'll be back in a bit to get you." He turns tail and leaves the room to do whatever doctors do in a situation like this.

Taking a deep breath, I try to focus my thoughts. I wish there was something I needed to do at this point, but really, it's all done. The nursery is ready to go. Rowen can pick up the car seat before we leave in a few days. HR already has the paperwork in motion for my maternity leave. There is literally nothing for me to do but sit and wait. It sucks.

"I'm gonna go ring yer mam," Ryan suddenly says. I forgot he was even here. "She'll want te be here."

Rowen nods in understanding. "Do ye want to call your mam too?"

Part of me wants to, just because I feel like I'm in freak-out mode, but the other part knows there is a real possibility she'll go into hysterics. "Let's wait. I think it would be better for her be excited after the fact than have to wait while I'm having major surgery."

"Good point."

He goes silent again, lost in his own thoughts, and it hits me that I've never asked him how he feels about all this. Not since the day we found out I was pregnant.

"Hey." I nudge him with my shoulder.

"Hmm." He looks over at me, almost like he forgot I was next to him for a moment.

"How are you feeling about all this?"

He smiles shyly and looks down at his lap. "I'm terrified."

"Why?"

"You're my best friend and you're about to have major surgery. I know rationally that nothing bad is going to happen, but it just makes me really… really…"

"Anxious."

"Exactly." He looks back over at me with what can only be described as love in his eyes. For just this one moment, it's just the two of us against the world again. It makes me feel like we can get through anything.

Wrapping my arms around him, there's nothing I can say. I'm not a surgeon. I've never done this before. All I can do is try to stay calm and trust that we're exactly where we need to be, and things are exactly how they should be. It's not something I've felt for a really long time, but something about everyday life being put on the back burner to power through this together makes me feel strong.

"I love you, Rookie."

He holds me tighter and murmurs, "I love you too."

We stay like that, wrapped in each other's arms for as long as we can, a family of two for the last time.

CHAPTER 24

Rowen

I have dreamed about this day for months. Thought about every scenario on how it could happen. Planned for any situation. Prepared myself in every possible way.

Except this one.

Not one part of me anticipated I'd be standing in the hallway of the hospital wearing drab green scrubs with a matching surgical cap, waiting to join my wife in an operating room. And yet here I am, and I'd be lying if I said I wasn't more nervous than I've ever been in my life.

It's not just the operation. Yes, that is my immediate concern. As much as I like Dr. Hermann, he's getting ready to cut Tiffany open and pull our son out through a gaping wound. I'm sure there's more to it than that, but it basically boils down to that, and it's scary. What if he cuts the wrong part and he can't stop the bleeding? What if he accidentally cuts my child? What if she gets a major infection? The horrific possibilities are terrifying.

Taking a breath to refocus my thoughts, I try to remember all the positives. Tiffany won't be struggling through labor anymore, and our son will be here.

Our *son*.

Mo mhac.

Even the overwhelming scent of antiseptic can't stop the smile that crosses my face at the thought of seeing him for the first time. I can't wait. More than I've dreamed about his birth, I've dreamed about him in general. What will he be like? Will he like playing soccer or will he be more artistic? Will he be a people-watcher like me or the life of the party like his mam? Will he have my eyes and his mother's hair? Will he need exorbitant amounts of sunscreen like I do?

Actually, I know the answer to that last one and make a mental note to start buying SPF 70+. With my genes, it's inevitable he'll turn into a lobster any time he goes outside if we're not careful.

"Mr. Flanigan?"

I look up at someone covered from head to toe in surgical gear. I know it's not Dr. Hermann, but beyond that, I have no idea. It could be our nurse or someone else. There's no real way to tell.

"Mr. Flanigan, we're ready for you."

Pushing off the wall, I follow her through a set of automatic sliding doors, following her instructions to put my mask over my nose and mouth. As soon as we step foot into the room, I spot Tiffany lying on the table, arms strapped down with a sheet held up, so she can't see past her chest.

I'm directed to sit in the rolling chair next to her head and immediately begin stroking her hair. She turns when she feels me, her eyes droopy.

"Hey, Rookie." I assume by the groggy look on her face she's been given a few more drugs than she had before.

"How ye feeling, mo ghrá?"

She smiles weakly. "I really like these drugs."

Chuckling, I can only respond with, "I bet. Much better than labor pains, aiy?"

She nods and closes her eyes, enjoying my touch. "You're nervous. I can tell by your accent."

"I am. Are ye as scared as I am?"

"I'm terrified," she breathes.

"We're almost done, *A ghrá.*"

All around us, people in full surgical gear are moving with a sense of purpose, setting things up, moving equipment here and there. It probably only takes moments, but to me it feels like a lifetime.

Finally, the one person I do recognize looks over the sheet, a headband with a light attached to his head. Even behind the mask, there's no hiding Dr. Hermann's smile.

"You two ready to have a baby?"

"Yes, please," Tiffany answers, slowly looking back up at him.

"Well let's do it." Looking up at the clock, Dr. Hermann announces, "It's August nineteenth, Four thirteen p. m. Let's get started."

My breathing picks up as I wait and watch. I can't see what's going on behind that sheet, and I'm not sure I want to. I'd love to see my son being born but seeing Tiffany's insides all over the table doesn't sound nearly as appealing to me. Instead, I focus on the look on Dr. Hermann's face. He's focused but not frazzled. People move around him methodically, but no one seems frantic.

All good signs that calm my nerves just a bit.

Tiffany seems to be watching as well. Suddenly her eyes go wide. "Oh! That feels weird."

"Yeah, you're gonna feel some pressure while we do this," Dr. Hermann responds cheerfully. "But we're almost there. A little bit of suction here, please," he says to the person standing next to him.

I watch as his arms twist this way and that way as he works. Then suddenly, he makes an announcement. "Here he is!" Sure enough, he pulls my boy right out of my wife and holds him up to show us. "I think it's safe to say, this is definitely your son."

Tiffany starts laughing at his joke because he's right. Even with all the goo on him, my son has a shock of red hair you can't miss. He doesn't seem to like it any more than I do as indicated by the wail that comes out of his pink, puffy lips. He's pale skin is splotched with red, just like happens to me when I've been exerting myself too much.

He's the most beautiful thing I've ever seen.

"Ye did it." I lean over and kiss Tiffany on the forehead through my mask as Dr. Hermann hands our son over to the nurse who takes him to another part of the room. "Yer a mam, Tiffany. I'm a dadaí."

A lone tear escapes down her cheek, and I find myself holding back my own tears and I rest my forehead on hers.

"I'm a dadaí."

The thoughts are overwhelming. I've never been this happy in my life, and I've only seen him for a split second. Lifting my head, I look around trying to catch another glimpse. Apparently, I'm not as subtle as I think I am.

"Would you like to see your son? You can go over there."

Nodding, I stand up and follow the person over to a small table where my son is lying down, clearly unhappy by being poked and prodded. I don't blame him. I wouldn't like if all my glory was on display in front of these strangers either.

"Can I... can I touch him?" I ask tentatively, not sure what I'm allowed to do right now.

"Absolutely," the person says. "And talk to him. Babies like familiar voices."

Slowly, I get closer, still in awe that I'm looking at my son. My *son*. It feels like I'm walking through a dream. Reaching down, I touch his tiny hand which immediately stretches and grabs my finger. The contact makes me suck in a breath. He's real. This is real. It's not a dream at all.

"Hello there, mo mhac. I'm yer da. Yer mam and I have been waiting for ye."

His tiny face loses the grimace, and it looks like he's turning his head, trying to find me. But surely that can't be the case, right?

"Lookie there," the nurse says, putting a cap on his head and rubbing with him a towel. "He knows your voice. See how calm he is now?"

"I'm right here, mhac. I'm not leaving ye."

A few short seconds later, he's bundled in a white blanket with pink and blue stripes and the nurse is picking him up, holding him out to me. "Would you like to hold your son?"

My eyes widen for just a moment, knowing my entire world is about to shift again. "Please."

Gently, she places my son in my arms, and I know I'll never be the same. He's the smallest thing I've ever held and the most precious. Part of me is afraid I'll drop him, but the other part knows I'll never let him fall. Nothing in the world matters more than him and his mam. Nothing.

"Can I go sit next to me wife?" I know my accent is strong right now, but I don't care. I'm absolutely overwhelmed with my love for this child. Nothing else is important.

"Of course. In fact, let's introduce him to his mommy, shall we?"

I nod, and we walk slowly over to Tiffany who I realize has been watching us this whole time. Meeting her gaze, my eyes fill up with tears again. This is my family. It's not just the two of us anymore. And it's perfect.

Sitting down gently, the nurse helps me situate the babe next to Tiffany, so she can nuzzle him. It's awkward, being that her arms are still strapped down. But she wastes no time kissing his sweet cheeks and whispering words of love to him. I wish my camera was out because this moment should be frozen in time, although I know it's forever frozen in my memory.

When the baby begins to fuss a little, he's situated back in my arms for me to gently rock. "It's okay, mhac. You can sleep now, *ceann beag.*"

"You've got a lot of Gaelic going on there, Rookie," Tiffany chides playfully, speaking slowly through the drugs.

I chuckle because she's right. "I can't seem t'help it. I'm a lil overwhelmed right now."

"Good overwhelmed, right?"

I glance up, making eye contact and holding it. "The best overwhelmed I've ever been. I love you so much."

"I love you too." Looking back down at our son, she adds, "I was thinking. What do you think about the name Cace?"

Cocking my head, I smirk. "How's it spelled?"

She smiles as she humors me. "C-A-C-E."

"Someone's been looking up traditional Irish names, I see."

"Maybe a little," she jokes, then turns serious again as she looks at our son. "It means observant and vigorous. Kind of like you with all your people-watching and doing the right thing. Things I want him to be."

Gazing down at my son, I consider her idea. "Cace Flanigan. A good, strong Irish name for a good, strong Irish boy."

"Cace *Rowen* Flanigan," she corrects me.

If it's possible for a heart to swell even more, mine just did. My son. Named after me.

Today is officially the best day of my life.

Tiffany

"I know you'll be here when you can, Mom," I say through FaceTime on my phone. "Really, all we're going to do for the next few weeks is sleep and eat anyway. Maybe bathe."

Stroking the top of my son's head, I watch as he suckles on my breast. Yes, the dull pain of breastfeeding is there, but that doesn't take away the surreal feeling of being a new mom. It's amazing.

"I know." My mom sighs. "I'm just mad at myself. Of all the times to fall down some steps and break an ankle, this is the worst."

I giggle lightly. "I still can't believe you did it at the gym."

"And right after my kickboxing class too! I had just shown everyone what a badass I am, and three steps took me out."

"Any muggers with ill intentions better beware of running into you in a back alley. Unless there are stairs involved."

"Well, hopefully in the next few weeks, the doctor will clear me for travel. Then I'll be on the first plane there."

"Sounds good to me." Baby Cace squeaks and pulls away from my breast, nuzzling his nose into my skin. I guess he's done eating. "I need to go now, Mom. The baby is done, and my delivery boy just got here."

I look up just as Rowen licks some green sauce off the pad of his thumb. He just got back from Chuy's where he got my favorite taquitos and chips with green sauce. It's the first craving I've had in the last several months, so he's indulging me by spreading it all out on my hospital table. He's also laughing at my mom's clumsiness.

She sighs, knowing I'm about to shut off the camera. "All right. Give that baby some kisses from his grandma."

"I will. And Mom"—I give her a pointed stare—"do not pass any pictures along to anyone."

She has the gall to look offended. "Tiffany, I would never do that."

"No, Mom. Don't forward the text along to your best friend. Don't give it to the newspaper to post an announcement. It stays in your hands only."

"I still don't understand why the newspaper gave your

wedding announcement to the internet. I didn't tell them to do that."

Rowen doesn't bother to hide his jeer this time. My mother will never get it. She's only in her early fifties, but she has no use for technology. She's like the last remaining hippie. It's annoying sometimes. Like right now.

"That's not how it works, Mom." Cace squeaks again, and I know he's getting uncomfortable. "But I'll have to explain it later. I need to go."

"All right, I love you, honey."

"Love you too. Bye, Mom."

Rowen snatches my phone from the bed where it's propped and quickly ends the call. "We're gonna see an unauthorized picture of the baby online by tomorrow, aren't we?"

"My luck, it'll be one of me breastfeeding and everyone will get to see my boob again," I grumble, as I try to maneuver the baby and the clasp of my nursing bra at the same time. Rowen saves me by taking Cace out of my hands, cooing to him quietly. Within seconds, the baby is back asleep and in the bassinet.

Pulling the rolling table to me, my mouth waters at the smell of all my favorite foods. There's so much to choose from, I can't decide where to begin. "Man, it's good to be able to eat again."

Sitting in the chair next to me, Rowen grabs one of the Styrofoam plates and digs in. "For me too."

Gotta love my husband. Because of my aversion to smells, he stopped cooking anything that would make me sick. It meant surviving on protein shakes at home and eating fast food in the car—not ideal for any athlete. But it was a sacrifice he was willing to make, and I love him all the more for it.

A quick knock on the door has us both looking up to see my in-laws walking in.

"Where's *mo garmhac? A grandpa* is here!" Ryan announces, heading straight for the bassinet, rubbing his hands together, excitement across his face.

Rowen jumps out of his chair and cuts Ryan off. "No dadaí. You know the rule. You have to wash your hands first."

Ryan is clearly appalled at being deflected. "A little germs aren't going to hurt him, mhac. Ye've got to toughin' him up."

Denise passes by them as they continue to squabble over whose theory on germs is more accurate. Regardless of who is right, my money is on Rowen winning this argument. His protective instincts are in high gear. That includes every nurse, doctor, or visitor who has walked into this room.

As I attempt to push my food aside, Denise pushes it back in front of me. "Don't stop eating because of us. You need your calories." She places a gift bag with an attached balloon on the table next to our food and sits down on the bed next to me, quickly watching how the fight is resolving. Like I predicted, Ryan throws his hands in the air and turns to the sink for a hand washing. "How are you feeling?"

"Let's see," I tick off my ailments on my fingers. "I can't laugh, or it hurts my incision. Nursing makes me feel like my uterus is going to explode. And mesh panties have to be the most uncomfortable form of undergarments I've ever worn."

She chuckles lightly. "So you're powering through your first few days of motherhood."

"Yep."

"When does Rowen go back to work?"

I sigh. This is the hardest part of his job. While I have eight weeks of maternity leave, Rowen doesn't get any. Times are changing, but athletes are held accountable for their professional responsibilities during the season, whether they're a first-time dad or not. Which means I'm already about to be on my own, and I'm scared shitless. Of course, I won't admit that to anyone.

"Tomorrow," is all I say. "Their next game sequence is in town, thank God. But I think they leave again next week."

Denise gives me a sympathetic look. If anyone knows how it feels to be left alone postpartum, it's her. "Is he going to be able to come home in the middle of the day, do you think?"

"I don't think he could stay away if he tried." Looking over at my husband who is hovering over his father as he holds our son, I have no doubt Rowen will be figuring out a way to stop by throughout the day.

Denise's face lights up when she realizes what I'm looking at. Grabbing her phone, she takes a quick stealth picture then leans over to show me.

"Look at that. Three generations of Flanigan men."

I stare at the moment in time she just captured. The way the sunlight streams in lights up their bright red hair, making all of them look practically angelic. The look of love on their faces as they gaze at our son, who is cooing back at them, melts my heart.

I'm the luckiest woman in the world.

EPILOGUE

Tiffany

"**K**eep doing that," I moan, grabbing Rowen's hair and pulling him closer to my core. His tongue still does magical things to my lady parts and today, he's going to town. Licking, nipping, and sucking as he inserts two fingers inside me, hitting just the right spot. "Oh, that's it. Right there… ohgod…"

My orgasm hits me fast and hard, just the way I like it these days.

He continues to suck on my clit as the waves overtake me, riding me to that sated feeling I love. But he's not done yet.

As soon as I've come back down to earth, he kisses up my body, paying special attention to the scar that now mars my abdomen. When I look at my stomach, I see flabby skin that hasn't tightened up yet and a knife wound. But Rowen tells me it's beautiful. That it's a reminder of the sacrifice I made to give him the best gift he's ever received—our son. Coming from anyone else, I'd say they were full of shit. But coming from Rowen, I know he means every word. Because of it, I still feel beautiful.

It also helps that my boobs grew three sizes and he can't stop looking at them.

Continuing his trek up my body, Rowen pauses to pull the cup of my nursing bra down a bit and kiss the tops of my breasts. He knows not to go any further. Sex, post baby is great. Getting the nursing boobs involved, though, it's not a good idea.

He pushes my thighs apart to settle in as he gently bites all the way up to the spot behind my ear. It's practically primal and gets my motor running again. Holding him to me, he thrusts inside, making me moan with pleasure once again. His hips move at a frantic pace, but it's too much.

Gently slapping his chest, I push him away. "Babe. Rowen, my scar."

He immediately pushes off me, knowing exactly what I'm implying. I love having sex with my husband. That has never changed. But even twelve weeks after Cace's birth, the friction of our bodies irritates that area. We've learned to make adjustments.

Situating himself on his knees, he yanks my body toward his, lining himself up with me again. Before he thrusts, though, he cocks his head and looks over to the side, listening.

"He's fine. He's still asleep. Get inside me, Rookie."

Turning his attention back on me, he complies with my demand. Only instead of thrusting, he goes slow, gaining traction and drawing out the anticipation of our pending orgasms as long as possible.

I stretch my arms above me and grab the headboard, hanging on for dear life as his gentle ministrations are short-lived and he ends up pounding into me, taking what he wants and giving me just as much in return.

"Ohgod, Rowen. I'm almost there..." I cry.

"Get there..." he pleads, and I know he's holding back, waiting for me.

Reaching between my legs, he pinches my clit ever so slightly and that's all that it takes to push me over the edge again.

"Oooooooooohhhhhhhh..." I call out, hoping I don't wake the baby who is in the bassinet across the room, but not able to control the sounds that come from deep within.

Very quickly, Rowen follows right behind me. "Fuck... me..."

Several very long and blissful seconds later, Rowen collapses next to me on the bed. We immediately roll into the spooning position and rest. I'm not quite sure how our sex life has remained intact with a newborn who doesn't sleep through the night, but it has. I suppose there is one benefit to having a C-section. As soon as my stitches were out, we were given the all clear to enjoy ourselves again, as long as we used some heavy-duty precautions against getting pregnant again so soon. The idea of going through another nine months of morning sickness scared the shit out of me, so I started a low dose pill that same day.

Gently running his hand over the scar my husband is fascinated with, Rowen asks, "Does it feel different? When you orgasm?"

Shifting into him, it takes me a second to decide how to answer. "A little. It sounds really unsexy to talk about."

"Humor me," he says with a kiss to my neck.

"You know physically when I orgasm, my entire uterus tightens up, right?"

"Mmhmm." More kisses.

"It's like I can feel where the incision was. It doesn't hurt or anything. It's just… I don't know. Maybe it's tighter? That's the only way I can describe it."

"But it still feels good?"

A smile crosses my face. Leave it to my husband to be worried about my orgasms being good enough. "You mean you can't tell by the look on my face?"

He chuckles. "Wow. It must feel really good with the way your eyes roll in the back of your head."

I smack him lightly making him laugh. It's good timing too. Cace starts shifting around and if the heavy feeling in my breasts is any indication, it's time to feed.

Before I even have to ask, Rowen is up and out of bed, crossing the room to pick up our son.

"Good morning, mo mhac. Are you ready for some lunch? Mam's got your milk all ready for you."

I smile at their one-sided conversations while I situate myself in bed, unclipping my nursing bra. Whoever thought to put clasps at the top of bra cups should win an award. It makes things so much easier.

Handing him to me, Rowen gives me a quick peck on the lips followed by a quick peck on the top of my breast. "Enjoy those while you can, little man. I'm taking them back in about nine months."

Cace gurgles and waves his fists, eyes locked in on his target. As soon as he latches on, I grimace, the familiar tightening in my chest as my milk lets down. Thankfully, it's short-lived, and very quickly, we relax into the moment.

Rowen makes sure we're all settled before kissing me on the top of the head and throwing on his sweats. "What do you want to eat? My mam brought bangers and mash."

"I'll leave that for you," I joke, knowing it's his favorite. "But do we still have any of that grilled chicken salad? I don't know why but it sounds really good."

"Yep. I'll go grab it for you."

The last three months have been an adjustment, but overall, it's gone really well. Cace is a great baby, but I didn't expect anything less with him being Rowen's child. Well, that's not exactly true. A part of me always remembered Ryan is his grandfather, so I know there's some ornery in there waiting to come out. But for the most part, he's very docile. Cries when he's hungry, fusses when he's wet, but otherwise even-tempered.

And my in-laws have been wonderful. Sure, the men argue all the time about the safest way to hold the baby or the best cleaning products. Denise and I just laugh at the ridiculousness and let them hash it out. In the end, as long as Cace is safe and happy, the rest is irrelevant anyway.

Having her nearby has worked out much better than I thought it would. She's very careful to not overwhelm us with her presence, but has been such a huge help, especially when Rowen is out of town.

The first time he had a series of away games, Cace was only a week old. I wasn't sure how I was going to manage on my own, but Denise was at my house every day at eight in the morning to clean the kitchen, make sure I ate, and take care of the baby when I napped. A few times she did a load of baby laundry. But mostly she fed me and helped me where I needed it. I'm grateful she did. People forget that a C-section is still major surgery, even if they send you home three days later. It was tough carrying a baby around or bending down to pick up something I dropped. That's where she came in. And with her gentle demeanor, it never felt imposing at all.

Ryan, on the other hand, had to be left at home a few times. Okay, that's a slight exaggeration. More like Denise didn't tell him she was coming over because he was a little too determined to build an indoor soccer goal in the baby's bedroom. Once the obsession passed, we let him come over again. I'm sure he's waiting for me to go back to work, so he can sneak in and complete the project.

Situating himself back on the bed next to me, Rowen spears some lettuce and chicken on a fork and holds it up to me. "Open," he demands, and I comply, taking a bite.

"Mmm. That hits the spot," I say around my chewing. "Thank you."

"No need to thank me. I'm just taking care of you." He takes his own bite, and searches around the bowl for more goodness to give us. "Are you ready for today?"

Taking another bite, I try to assess how I feel. It's been three months since I've been at work, and while I'm excited to get back to my job, I'm torn up inside about leaving my baby behind. I was planning to only take eight weeks but couldn't bear the thought of leaving him that soon. I didn't expect to feel that way. I'm more comfortable now. Probably because I'm leaving him with Denise, the person who loves him the most after me and Rowen. I strongly believe having adult role models of various ages will be good for my son, but that doesn't mean I'm not a tiny bit jealous of my mother-in-law for getting to be with him. Which is ridiculous, considering I've been with him non-stop for twelve weeks. And nine months before that if you count the time before he was evicted out of my body.

"I think I am," I finally admit. "It's going to be weird at first, but I'll be fine."

Rowen looks at me, snatching a small piece of lettuce off the fork, and clearly assessing my mood.

"What?" I break from his gaze, as I shift Cace to the other side, but I know Rowen is still watching me. I can practically feel his eyes on me.

"You trust me, right?"

Furrowing my brows, I look at him like he's lost his mind. "What kind of question is that?"

"I just wanna make sure you're not worried something is going to happen while you're gone, or that I'm not going to notice if he needs something."

I small laugh bursts out of me. "Rowen, you are the last person I'm worried about not noticing if he needs something. You're a bit of a helicopter parent already."

His jaw drops in mock incredulousness. "I am not."

"You were cheering him on when he pooped the other day," I deadpan.

"He was constipated! I was giving him encouragement. That can be painful."

"Whatever you say." I snatch the fork from his hand and make a show of getting as much salad on it as I can. "It was funny at this age, but if you do things like that when this kid is ten, I'm going to start calling you by your dad's name since that's the type of shit he'd do."

"Tiffany! Language!"

Pointing the fork at him, I rest my case. "And there's the sound of the rotors now!"

He snatches the fork from me again, grumbling about

how he's always loved air travel or something I'm only half listening to. The baby has fallen asleep, which is good timing. I have to get ready for work anyway or I'm going to be late.

"What time do you go back to the stadium?" Quickly, I shift Cace onto the bed, grabbing a tiny diaper off the nightstand next to me.

"I have to be back at two," Rowen says, as he eyes the breast I'm working on covering up. Perv.

"What time does the game start?"

"Four. I wish you could be there."

I grab his cheeks and give him a big smack on the lips before handing off my son and climbing out of bed, Rowen swatting my rear as I go. "I know. Me too. But I'll be cheering for you from my office. If you're lucky, I might even ogle your ass," I say over my shoulder, making him laugh, as I walk confidently to the bathroom for a shower. Time to balance motherhood and career.

———————

The snick of the lock unlatching when I wave my key fob in front of the door is the first real sign that life is going back to normal. Well, as normal as life can be after a new little human has come into the world. But as I step through the door and into the newsroom, I realize nothing has changed.

The scanners are still squawking. Reporters are still making calls and typing. Televisions still glow with every local station and CNN ready to be monitored. The only difference is the person at the assignment desk.

"Hi Tom," I greet as I grab a huge stack of mail I'll need to sort through upstairs. There's too much to go through down here.

"Tiffany." He tips his head at me and goes back to his business. Tom took over for Caleb when he moved upstairs. He's a little older than everyone else in the newsroom. His hair and neatly trimmed beard are almost gray. He's pleasant enough, just sticks to himself. We definitely don't have the same kind of rapport Caleb and I use to have.

That also means I don't waste any time heading to my office. Caleb is already there, setting up. When he notices me walk in, his face lights up. "Tiffany!" There's no hesitation when he gives me a strong hug. "Welcome back! We've missed you!"

"Thanks. I've missed being here. Anything exciting happening today?"

I lay my bags on the floor and carefully toss the mail onto my desk. I'm already dreading how many emails I'm going to have to go through.

"Sunday Night Football, obviously. And then of course the Mutiny game."

I nod. "Good. Are we going to have a camera out there today?"

"Yep. Nothing terribly exciting is happening in the news world, so Mannie and Jerold are already out doing pre-game interviews and getting some b-roll for the five o'clock show."

"Awesome." Reaching into my bag for supplies, I grab the most important thing first—a small picture frame. Inside is a picture of my family of three at the hospital. Rowen and I are sitting on the bed, Cace in my arms. All three of us are wearing beanies. We decided if Cace was getting pictures taken with a hat on, we could make it a family thing. It's my favorite picture of us and immediately goes next to my monitor, where I'll see it all day every day.

"What's the extra bag for?" Caleb inquires. I know he's about to regret asking, though.

I look him dead in the eye, not wanting to miss his reaction. "That's my breast pump."

The grimace he makes has me laughing out loud at the over the top expression. "Why did you tell me that? You could have lied to me."

"That wouldn't have been very fun," I say, wiping a tear from my eye.

"At least tell me you won't be using it in front of me."

I give him a pointed look. "Now, Caleb. Breastfeeding is a natural thing. You wouldn't hate it if I just randomly whipped out my boobs for fun, would you?"

He opens his mouth to deny it, then thinks better of it and shrugs in agreement.

"Exactly. So you need to get over it. But," I continue, "I can also respect that it's going to take you a minute to not be squeamish, so don't worry. I'll find a cubicle somewhere to pump."

"Thank you." He sounds way too relieved for a grown man who likes boobs in general. He won't be relieved after my baby brain kicks in. I have to change out my nursing pads throughout the day, and sometimes I won't realize they end up on his chair. Hell, I put the silverware in the fridge last night. No telling what will happen when I'm trying to multi-task.

I shrug to myself at how fun this could end up being. Then I get right down to work.

Three hours later, we're watching the Texas Mutiny dominate over New England. It's only the first half and already we're up two to nothing. Daniel has been unstoppable today. If they keep this up, we're going to the playoffs.

Just as Rowen runs by, my phone dings with a text. It's from Denise and has a picture of my baby grinning up at her.

Just want you to know we're doing fine and watching Daddy play soccer. Have a great day at work!

I run my fingers over the picture of his little face and save it to my phone before dropping the device back on my desk. The picture frame I put out a couple hours ago catches my attention, and I have one of those moments where life is surreal.

I'm watching my husband on television as he kicks ass at his dream job.

I'm sitting here kicking ass at my own dream job.

And my mother-in-law is spending some coveted time with my baby, making sure he's happy and healthy and loved.

It was a struggle to get here, but I really can have it all.

Nailed it.

THE END

ACKNOWLEDGMENTS

Laurie Darter – You get the very first acknowledgement because Ryan wouldn't be what he is without you. And he's so fun. Thank you for your never-ending knowledge of an Irish immigrant's dialect. And thank your family, too, for being stubborn and cussing a lot in Gaelic around you! Lol

Megan Addison – I could not have made it through this release without you. Seriously. You are a gem and the best thing that ever happened to Andrea, which is how I found you. So thank you for all the organization and for talking me off the proverbial ledge.

Andrea Johnston – I could thank you for a lot of things, but I think this sums it up: thank you for sharing Megan.

Stacey Grice, Marisol Scott, Kate Spitzer, Katie Pettigrew – Thank you all for keeping me organized, making sure the details of this book were correct, finding plot holes, etc. You ladies are the best!

Erin Noelle, Karen Lawson, Julie Titus – Thank for you for putting the shine on this baby! I think it turned out fabulous.

Murphy Rae – Nailed it. HA! See what I did there???

Mom – Since when have you been such a good proofreader? Thanks for doing the last minute once over! And you're welcome for teaching you sex scene terminology.

Carter's Cheerleaders – My friends, my smart asses, my biggest fans. You guys brighten my day every day. Thank you for keeping it real and keeping me sane.

The Walk – You know who you are. You know why you're important. I love you ladies so much, it's unreal. You are the biggest blessing I've had in this community. Keep walking the good walk, sisters.

Thank you, God, for sticking with me through the hard, hard days. I can see that light at the end of the tunnel. I'll keep putting one foot in front of the other and trust you got the rest.

And thank you Tiffany and Rowen for being the last couple I expected to discover while sitting in my car during dance practice, researching derogatory terms for the word "groupie". Never in my wildest dreams could I expect a story could turn my world upside down, change my perspective on how I look at others, and provide such massive amounts of wisdom we should all adhere to. You turned a single book about a soccer player into a series that helped me process through my own hard times. It's been a fun, sometimes stressful ride. And it's been worth every second.

GO TEXAS MUTINY!

ABOUT THE AUTHOR

Mother, reader, storyteller—ME Carter never set out to write books. But when a friend practically forced a copy of Twilight into her hands, the love of the written word she had lost as a child was rekindled. With a story always rolling around in her head, it should come as no surprise that she finally started putting them on paper. She lives in Texas with her four children, Mary, Elizabeth, Carter and Bug, who sadly was born long after her pen name was created, and will probably need extensive therapy because of it.

You can follow her on Facebook at
https://www.facebook.com/authorMECarter,
on Twitter at https://twitter.com/AuthorMECarter,
Instagram at authorMECarter
(https://www.instagram.com/authormecarter/?hl=en)
or email her at AuthorMECarter@gmail.com

Other Titles by M.E. Carter

Hart Series

Change of Hart
Hart to Heart
Matters of the Hart

Texas Mutiny Series

Juked
Groupie
Goalie
Megged

#MyNewLife Series

Getting a Grip
Balance Check
Pride & Joie
Amazing Grayson

www.ingramcontent.com/pod-product-compliance
Lightning Source LLC
Chambersburg PA
CBHW070634170726
48291CB00003B/1017